A GASTRONOMIC MURDER

A GASTRONOMIC MURDER

ALEXANDRA ROUDYBUSH

PUBLISHED FOR THE CRIME CLUB BY

DOUBLEDAY & COMPANY, INC.

GARDEN CITY, NEW YORK

1973

All of the characters in this book
are fictitious, and any resemblance
to actual persons, living or dead,
is purely coincidental.

ISBN: 0-385-03926-3
Library of Congress Catalog Card Number 73–79707
Copyright © 1973 by Alexandra Roudybush
All Rights Reserved
Printed in the United States of America
First Edition

To Clover

who wished I'd give recipes for some of the dishes I describe in my book, so I did.

CHAPTER I

Prince Ottokar von Altberg-Emringen, slowly dying in a sanatorium in the Black Forest, had been profoundly relieved when he learned that the Schloss Altberg had been taken over by the American Army. Now he could feel that the family heritage was safe. The war years had been long and weary for the old prince: his only son had been taken prisoner on the Russian front and might never return, but he was able to take comfort in the fact that his pretty American daughter-in-law, with her three sons, was safely in America; the proud line of Altberg-Emringen was not threatened with extinction.

Most of that string of castles that had formed the Maginot Line (except that it was effective) of the Middle Ages were now picturesque ruins, but the Schloss Altberg, while as picturesque as any of them, was far from a ruin. It was, in fact, the epitome of solid comfort, boasting, as it did, bathrooms, kitchens, central heating, and even a tiny elevator. It also boasted a collection of over two hundred French Impressionist paintings.

All this was due to the Prince Ottokar's grandfather, who, faced with a crumbling castle and a mountain of debt, decided that money was more important than quarterings and cast about for a wealthy wife. After canvassing the field, he selected the only child of an automobile manufacturer, then a nascent industry but one which he felt had enormous potential. Anyway, she was prettier than any of the other possibles. His shrewd foresight was rewarded: gold poured into the Altberg-Emringen coffers and he and his wife delightedly spent it, he on his paintings, which he picked up for nearly nothing, and she on a collection of jewels that rivaled that of any royal family and included two necklaces, one the property of Marie Antoinette and one, with matching tiara, earrings, and bracelet, that of Catherine of Russia.

The family fortune, between the two world wars, had seriously declined, but, Prince Ottokar reflected, his grandmother's wild extravagance and his grandfather's taste in art were left as a basis on which to rebuild the fortune of the House of Altberg-Emringen. The old prince turned his face to the wall and died.

* * *

Major George Zillitch, of the Quartermaster Corps, was filled to overflowing with a sense of well-being as he gazed while shaving at the somewhat plump face reflected in the mirror over the Meissen washbasin. The taps represented dolphins, beautifully executed, one in gold and one in silver, out of whose respective mouths hot and cold water spouted. The toilet, also of Meissen, was encased in gleaming mahogany with a mahogany-covered overhead tank and the cord to flush it was of entwined gold and silver ending in a tassel.

War, he reflected as he climbed down the alabaster steps that led into the alabaster tub, might have been hell for some people. For him, it had proved to be life's golden opportunity and, as he lay back in happy euphoria, he thought with pleasure of his nest egg, foresightedly established in a Swiss bank, steadily getting larger. If the Occupation lasted another two years or, with luck, three, he'd have enough to start in business for himself, perhaps even here in Germany. A country that has to build itself up again after destruction always offers opportunities to the get-rich-quick brigades.

The only cloud on his horizon was the increasing frequency of Edna Mae's talk regarding the advantages of matrimony and vague references to possible pregnancy. The last few days there had even been a menacing undertone to her remarks.

Of course, in finding outlets for the china, glass, carpets, and furniture he had "liberated" over the past two years, Edna Mae had been of tremendous use to him, he reflected as he dried himself before the triple mirror with a bath sheet embroidered with the arms of the House of Altberg-Emringen ("Gosh, I've *got* to lose weight," he said to himself as he noted that his waistline had completely disappeared and that his buttocks jiggled as he moved), but now that he had a firm contact in Colonel O'Hara's wife, who was the owner of a fashionable antique store in Houston, he really no longer needed Edna Mae. Mrs. O'Hara simply gave him lists of the things she wanted for her store, and these would ultimately be shipped back to Texas at the taxpayers' expense. On her return to Houston, she expected to have the second best antique store in the United States. The second best because the wife of General Kinkaid, who also was in the antique business, had a larger group of searchers and, of course, could pull rank on her.

Major Zillitch and his WAC assistant had hoped that the Schloss Altberg would offer unlimited opportunities for profitable transactions, but it had been disappointing. The paintings, which were the most valuable art objects in the schloss, were all inventoried, as were most of the tapestries and carpets, and the caretaker of the castle had insisted on going through the place, room by room, with George and Edna Mae. In the first few months after the war it might have been possible to loot the place with impunity but now it would be dangerous for anyone but a professional art thief, who would have the necessary contacts to dispose of his "acquisitions."

For the rest, most of the furniture (which was uninventoried) was too dark and heavily carved for American taste and also too large for American homes. Stag antlers, of which there was a plethora, were unsalable and, while George rather liked the Biedermeier with which one wing was furnished, Mrs. O'Hara turned thumbs down. (Actually, she was to regret this —Biedermeier later became very fashionable in the States.)

Still, George had not done too badly. There were some rugs and tapestries, as well as sets of Nymphenberg and Rosenthal that did not appear on the inventory, and plenty of odd bibelots and figurines. Mrs. O'Hara was particularly delighted by their find, in a drawer, of a collection of magnificent jeweled icons, probably looted from Russia by the son of the house and brought home by him on one of his leaves from the Eastern Front.

All in all, they made about seven thousand dollars from the

Schloss Altberg. George Zillitch was looking forward to his next assignment, now that the schloss was ready to receive the senior officers and their families, for whom it had been taken over to provide a place of rest and relaxation for them to recover from the effects of the never-ending round of cocktail parties they gave for each other.

George was an adopted child and, having watched his foster parents work an eighteen-hour day trying to keep a small grocery store going during the Depression years, decided there must be easier ways to earn a living and headed for New York. Rather taken with the idea of a uniform, he managed to get a job as a bellboy in one of the city's lesser hotels, and it was here that he first learned how to make a quick buck.

At the end of six months, he was on to all the gimmicks. While he procured (both alcohol and sex) and helped drunks to bed (and himself to their money), he was willing, efficient, and likable. By 1939 he had worked his way to the Waldorf as elevator operator and finally was promoted to desk clerk. In this position his salary was considerably better than that of an elevator operator, of course, but his income plummeted until he discovered the gold mine of the hotel room shortage. War had come to Europe and New York was chockablock with purchasers of munitions and other war equipment, those with sufficient means to flee the discomforts and dangers of life in Europe, government spokesmen and pseudo government spokesmen, other VIPs and crooks. It was, he found, a simple matter to reserve rooms under a fictitious name and then allocate them, in exchange for greenbacks the value of which frequently exceeded by a multiple the price of the room, to the desperate hordes that besieged the hotel every day.

Hearing that the takings were even better in the nation's capital, where the five-day limit on the stay of a guest kept the poor things wandering from hotel to hotel, George Zillitch moved there after Pearl Harbor. What had been frenzy in New York became hysteria in Washington. The town was swamped. Some of the visitors were genuinely prompted by patriotism and the desire to do something for the war effort, but for the most part those who descended on the town consisted of seekers of jobs, commissions, contracts, excitement, and/or husbands. Here the room clerk was king, and generals, statesmen, admirals, and millionaires sued for his favors and trembled at his frown. The grapevine soon spread the news that, provided you made it worth his while, George Zillitch was the man to see if you needed somewhere to lay your head.

George was very content. Not only was his wallet well stuffed, but, of equal importance to him, so was his stomach. The steaks, butter, bacon, scotch, and brandy lesser mortals had to do without were readily available to him. He realized, however, that, since he was healthy, single, young, and not in what by any stretch of the imagination could be called a job vital to the war effort, Uncle Sam would inevitably be breathing down his neck. The idea of a snappy uniform with suitable shoulder bars had its appeal, but George's whole soul revolted at the idea of life in the ranks. A commission in the Quartermaster Corps would, he thought, be the least painful way of fighting for flag and country, and he began to pay particular attention to the various generals who registered at the hotel, going out of his way to be friendly and agreeable to these warriors.

This ploy bore fruit. Through the efforts of General F. T. C. Brown, whom he provided with unlimited quantities of Haig & Haig pinch bottle and two dozen pairs of nylons, he became a lieutenant in the Quartermaster Corps, his years of hotel experience serving in lieu of any form of higher education.

George's uniform was spandy-new when he and a friend with whom he shared an apartment decided to go to the theater. After the show George suggested they stop at O'Donnell's for a late snack.

"The pies there are sensational," George said. "They've got a rum pie that's out of this world, and O'Donnell's is the only place where I've ever had a pumpkin pie that didn't have a soggy crust. I don't know how they do it."

At the restaurant, they sat at a table next to two WACs who were downing boilermakers like good 'uns. After a little cross-table kidding the two young men moved over to join the girls.

George, a hearty eater rather than any kind of a drinker, never had any very clear recollection as to what happened after his third boilermaker. When he woke up, he was alone in his own bed with a skull-splitting headache and a heaving stomach. He could hear someone taking a shower in the bathroom and hoped whoever it was would be out before his own needs became acute. A few minutes later a naked female strolled into the bedroom and began to dress. With a muttered apology, George brushed past her into the bathroom and locked the door. When he finally emerged, white and shaken, the stranger was neatly dressed, with every hair in place. She glanced at him with amused sympathy.

"I gotta get back by seven," she said. "Why don't you get some more sleep? I'd make you a prairie oyster if I had time. You'll be all right later, kid."

"Where's Tom?" George muttered.

"He and Lucy went to her place. Her pa's rich and she's got a real cute apartment out Sixteenth Street. Well, so long, kid. Hope you feel better."

"Wait! I don't know your name."

The WAC paused, her hand on the doorknob.

"It's Edna Mae Jones."

"Where can I get in touch with you? I owe you an apology."

"Forget it. I'm shipping out next week. I don't know your name, either, but that doesn't faze me. Toodle-oo, stranger."

After she had gone, George followed her suggestion and went back to sleep. When he woke up, as Edna Mae had prophesied, he felt almost human.

In 1946, George Zillitch, now a captain, was sitting at his desk when he was told that his new WAC assistant was reporting for work. When she came in and saluted, George had no idea he'd ever seen her before.

It was not until she said, "Sergeant Edna Mae Jones reporting for duty, sir," that he suddenly realized who she was.

The two stared at each other.

"Say, aren't you the guy—"

"O'Donnell's, in Washington," George replied.

"Gee, that's right." Edna Mae grinned. "Well, don't let it bother you none. I'd forgotten all about it."

George, feeling vaguely insulted, looked at Edna Mae with interest. He had remembered her as being somewhat plump, but army life had slimmed her down and her figure almost made up for her moon face, thick lips, and wary black eyes. There was no getting around the fact that the girl was homely.

"God! I must have been drunk," George reflected.

However, Edna Mae turned out to be a pretty good assistant. At first, George kept their relations highly formal and she followed his example.

It was not until they found themselves alone together in a vast, empty hotel in the Bavarian Alps that the situation changed. They had come to see what needed to be done to convert the place into a vacation spot for U. S. Army personnel. It had been shut up for two years and was damp, cold, and depressing.

A miserable dinner was prepared by a sullen old woman who lived next door and had let them in and turned the keys reluctantly over to them. George tried to build a fire but the wood was wet and, far from giving heat, it merely filled the room with smoke. Edna Mae got the makings out of her bag and fixed several hot toddies. They finally went to bed together more for warmth than from irresistible impulse. To George's surprise, he found Edna Mae the best jump he'd ever had.

During the two months they were together refitting the hotel, George and Edna Mae came to a tacit understanding. Each, separately, had gone in for a little larceny, George chiefly through traffic in coffee and cigarettes, to which he had unlimited access, in exchange for china, glass, silver, and modest jewelry, for which he found ready outlets, while Edna Mae had worked for the most part with nylons, beauty products, and various intimate hard-to-get feminine necessities. She had, she told him, a lengthy list of prospective clients and their respective desires. These, she thought, could be better satisfied by merely lifting the wanted objects from the various private houses they were constantly requisitioning for the use of the rapidly expanding army of bureaucrats pouring into Germany to guzzle at the trough of Military Government.

On the whole, George agreed that purloining what they needed was perhaps less dangerous than traffic in illicit booze and so forth, though he was shaken when he learned of a thirty-thousand-dollar killing in whiskey made in one month by a British Army colleague.

So the partnership was set up and business boomed. They saw to it that the homes the Army requisitioned had wealthy owners and, while at first they had been discreetly light-fingered, as time went by and they realized it would be hard to prove which of the stream of military and civilian personnel who were assigned the various places had actually taken what was missing, they became more and more acquisitive. George secreted his sizable savings in a Swiss bank, slipping over to Geneva from time to time. He never inquired what Edna Mae did with her share of the loot, and she never mentioned it.

* * *

George Zillitch spread a cover on the floor and glumly began the exercises the doctor whom he had consulted about his rapidly increasing embonpoint had prescribed.

"Of course," the latter said, "all the exercises in the world won't help if you don't cut down on your eating." And he scribbled out an appropriate diet for George to follow.

"But I'll starve!" the latter exclaimed, scanning it.

"Precisely," the doctor replied.

The effect of the diet, for the few days that he stuck to it, was to make George very, very cross, and the exercises merely made him crosser. It was while he was lying on his back, trying to get to a hundred bicycle strokes with his legs in the air, that he fell sideways. There was a strange sound and George, when he had righted himself and massaged his bruises, got up to see what he had hit. A door, where no door had been, had swung open and revealed a steel safe. George stood looking at it, mouth agape. It was an old safe, painted black and decorated with wreaths of roses and pink cherubs. George Zillitch had forced more than one safe during his years in Germany, and this one looked like duck soup. From a drawer, he took a little leather case of tools and set to work. At the end of an hour's intensive work, the door swung open to reveal shelves lined with boxes. Taking them out in the light, he opened one after another in mounting excitement. There were necklaces, tiaras, crescents, coronets, bracelets, rings, and brooches set in diamonds, emeralds, rubies, and every kind of precious stone which sparkled and gleamed. There were chests of silver that contained candelabra, bowls, and tableware of all descriptions as well as a complete vermeil service for twenty-four people. There were chessmen the like of which George had never seen: sixteen pieces were set in pearls and the other sixteen in dark rubies. And, when George opened a chamois bag, he found it held diamonds of all sizes and shapes.

Suddenly George heard a sound behind him and he whipped around in anger. In his agitation he had forgotten to lock his door, had forgotten he was buck naked, had forgotten Edna Mae, who now advanced into the room and gazed at the jewels, spread all over the vast bed and tables, chests, chairs.

"My God!" she whispered, in awe.

George clenched his fists and closed his eyes as he forced himself to master the fury her inopportune arrival had aroused, directed as much at himself as at her. Not trusting himself to speak, he went over to lock the stable door before any other horses could come in. Then he put on his robe and slippers and lit a cigarette with a shaking hand.

"Quite a haul!" he managed to croak, after a few puffs.

She looked up at him, white with excitement.

"Where did it come from?"

George pointed to the safe.

"And it isn't on that damn inventory, either!" Edna Mae said.

"I suppose they thought it was safely hidden."

"What are we going to do?"

It was the "we" that brought George up short.

"I'll have to think about it," he said carefully. "We'll have to put them back now." He glanced at his watch. "General Urquart and Colonel Waleweski will be here in half an hour."

"Oh, George, I'll die if I don't put all this stuff on! I'll never have a chance like this again. I want to see what it feels like to be a princess," and she glanced up at the portrait of the Princess von Altberg-Emringen. Mellen had painted her in a white taffeta ball gown, wearing the set of emeralds Edna Mae now held in her hands.

"Don't be a fool!" George said shortly. A mutinous look came over Edna Mae's pudding face, a look George had come to know only too well. "There isn't time now," he added hastily. "I've got to get dressed before those ginks get here. Beat it."

"I'll put the stuff away while you dress."

"Beat it, I said!"

"What's eating you?"

"Hell, what do you think's eating me? This is something I've got to think through very carefully. I can't afford to make any mistakes."

"'We,'" Edna Mae amended. "All this made me clean forget what I came to tell you. It'll be a case of 'Just Mollie and me, and baby makes three' in about seven months. I had some tests done and the results were positive." George stood as though paralyzed.

There was a sound of a car coming up the long hill to the schloss and Edna Mae glanced out the window. "Oh, God! Here they are. I'll go on down and tell them you've been delayed for a few minutes. So long, daddy!"

After she had gone, George forced himself jerkily to restore the jewels to their hiding place. When he came to the chamois bag with the loose stones, he hesitated. Edna Mae, dazzled by the set jewels, had not noticed this. Shoving it inside the case containing his toilet articles, he locked it in a valise, carefully checked the working of the secret door to make sure he could open it again without difficulty, and, throwing his clothes on, he hurried downstairs.

General Urquart and Colonel Waleweski were pleasantly commendatory about the schloss and the preparations made to receive the VIPs for whom it had been requisitioned. They were even more lavish with their praise of the excellence of the cooking and the high quality of the wines. George's career in the Army in fact had been considerably furthered by his own love of good food. Today, however, he had no appetite. After his superiors had finally left, George, telling Edna Mae he'd been called to Frankfurt, got in his car and drove off.

There was a pine forest about twenty miles north where Edna Mae and he had picnicked on several occasions and here George drove, stopped the car, and, lighting a cigarette, leaned back and set his mind to working as it had never worked before. A pack and a half later, he had drawn up his plan of action. Briskly, he started the car and drove back to the schloss.

That evening to Edna Mae he was loving, gentle, and thoughtful. He told her how happy he was about the baby, promised to take the necessary steps toward marriage, and, lying on his bed, watched while she excitedly tried on jewel after jewel. Since they were not exactly set off by the way she was dressed, even though she was out of uniform, George, lying on the bed and watching her, began to laugh.

"Oh, George," she said, hurt.

"Take all your clothes off and then put on the jewelry. There's a famous painting in a museum in Basel of Diane de Poitiers, naked, trying on jewels in front of a mirror. And your figure is so lovely, my darling."

"It won't be for long," Edna Mae replied as she undressed. "That is better," she remarked, surveying herself in Marie Antoinette's necklace. At the end of two hours, she was tired and, stripping herself of a three-strand pearl necklace and a diamond bracelet, carefully set them back in their cases, and joined George on the bed.

"What are we going to do, George?" she asked as she lay in his arms.

"When did you say the baby was coming?" he asked.

"The doctor said I was about two months along."

"We'd better get married as soon as we can, then," George said. "I'll talk to the padre and start the ball rolling right away."

"And what about the jewelry?"

"I've been thinking about that and there's only one man I

know who can help us. I met Jack Venturian when I was working at the Waldorf. In fact, I did a little business with him—a matter of a pretty good diamond ring I found in one of the rooms. The beauty about Jack is that he's a damn good working jeweler—he can do all his own cutting and resetting—and, in addition, he has his own swank store in Fifth Avenue, which gives him an outlet. What we've got to do is get that jewelry to Jack as soon as we can."

"How'll we do that?"

George lit a cigarette and lay back, blowing smoke rings.

"There's one way," he said slowly, "and that's— Oh, no I can't let you take such a risk."

"What is it, George? Tell me!"

"No, I won't. I'll think of something else."

"Please tell me."

"Well," George said reluctantly. "What I thought of was this. Supposing, instead of getting married here, with all the red tape and so forth, we both ask for leave and slip off to England. After we've had a short honeymoon we'll come back, announce our marriage and your pregnancy, and say you want out. You'll be flown back to the States."

"And I could take the jewelry with me!"

"I don't like to have you take the risk," George demurred.

"Of course I'll take the risk. Nobody ever looks through our luggage, particularly on a 'pregnancy' plane! That's much the easiest way of getting the things out! Then when I get to New York, I'll turn the things over to this Venturian. But do you think you can trust him?"

George shrugged.

"In one sense, yes. He's in the business. Of course, we won't get anything like what the things are worth. But from my previous experience with him, I figure he'll give us a cool million, and that's about the best we can do."

Edna Mae turned to her lover. "Oh, George! We'll be rich!" she whispered. "Rich, rich, rich!"

"Be quiet!" he ordered as he pulled her urgently toward him, his mouth hard on hers.

As they dressed the next morning, they talked over the plans. Then George opened a small velvet box containing a large marquise solitaire.

"How about this as an engagement ring?" he asked casually.

"Oh, George! Do you think . . . ?"

"Why not? But you'd better wear it on a chain around your neck, until we're married and home." And he slipped the ring on her finger.

"Isn't it beautiful?" she breathed.

George looked among the boxes.

"There was a real pretty small pearl necklace . . . oh, here it is." And he opened an oblong case in which lay the gleaming, evenly graduated pearls. "You could even *use* this for the wedding—nobody except experts can tell the difference between real and cultured pearls."

Edna Mae went back to her room in seventh heaven as she took with her the ring and the necklace. George watched her go with a grin on his face.

Edna Mae, on George's instructions, requested leave, which was granted. At the airport, as they were about to fly to London, George's name was boomed over the loudspeaker system and he went to answer a telephone call. A few moments later, he hurried back.

"That was General Urquart," he said. "He wants me to check on a shortage at the Darmstadt commissary right away. It'll only take a couple of days. You go on, Edna Mae. I'll join you Wednesday."

"Why don't I just wait?"

"Because I want you to take care of the preliminaries for our marriage—make what arrangements you can without me. Then there won't be any delay. Hurry if you're going to make the plane."

"Soon?" she murmured as he kissed her goodbye.

"Very, very soon!" he promised.

When she had gone, George drove back to the schloss, slipped on some gloves, and, opening the safe, removed all the jewelry from their velvet and tooled-leather cases and spread the pieces out on the bed. The silverware and the chess set he left in the safe. For some time he gazed at the two key pieces, the sets that had belonged to Marie Antoinette and Catherine of Russia. They were so beautiful and he knew that if he took them they would be broken up and lovely work would be lost. Finally, cursing himself for a sentimental fool, he put them back in their cases, which he restored to the safe. He also returned the empty cases. He then wrapped the various items up in underwear and socks, put them in his laundry bag, stuffing the top over with soiled shirts and pajamas. He carried a suitcase and the laundry bag down to his car and drove to Geneva.

Two days later he was in London and his marriage to Edna Mae in the Chelsea Registrar's office took place several days later.

Edna Mae was utterly happy. Clothes were still rationed in England, but she had managed to get together some sort of a trousseau.

"There's not any point in my getting much," she told George. "Because in a couple of months I'm not going to be able to wear anything I have now, anyway. Do you think I look nice?" And she pirouetted in her starched beige lace wedding dress.

"You know how I like you," he grinned at her. "Well, let's get going." And, with a bow, he handed her the bouquet he had bought. After the ceremony, they left for a leisurely motor tour of England. The weather was particularly fine that summer and the beaches of Devonshire and Cornwall particularly inviting, especially to Edna Mae, who loved the water. It was in a secluded little cove, near St. Ives, that tragedy struck.

As George was to testify at the inquest later, he and Edna Mae had picnicked on the beach and, after a lunch of meat pasty, strawberries, and saffron cake, he had fallen asleep. When he woke up, there was no sign of his wife. He tried to walk along the beach to see if he could find her, but the tide had come in making this impossible. Her cigarettes, sunglasses, and tote bag were by the picnic basket, as were her espadrilles and the garment she slipped on over her bikini.

After about half an hour had passed, George testified, he began to worry. Thinking that she might be stranded by the tide in one of the neighboring coves, he put on a sweater and a pair of sneakers and struggled up the little path, now the only exit from the beach, to the top of the cliff, hoping to catch sight of her. He called her name repeatedly, but there was no answer. When two young hikers with rucksacks on their backs came along, he asked them to go for help.

Edna Mae's body was found three days later, wedged between two rocks, five miles down the coast where it had been carried by the current. Death, the autopsy revealed, had been due to drowning and had occurred about an hour after the ingestion of meat and potato pasty, strawberries, and saffron cake. The victim had been pregnant at the time of the accident and the coroner expressed his deepest sympathy for the doubly bereaved husband.

George arranged for his wife's cremation, then returned to Germany to wind up her affairs. She had left no will but it was found that she allotted part of her pay to her widowed mother. In going through her papers George found a bankbook showing a balance of over thirty thousand dollars. He signed a waiver of any claim in her estate, arranging to have her effects packed and shipped to Passaic, where her mother lived. Then he flew back to the United States with the urn containing his late wife's ashes, to give his mother-in-law an account of the tragedy.

He found this task even more difficult than he had anticipated. Mrs. Jones, far from reproaching him for her only child's death, tried to forget her own grief to comfort her son-in-law for what she thought must be his even greater sorrow. She showed him albums full of pictures of her daughter at every stage of her development, pressing duplicates, of which there were many, on him; she talked about the girl and begged him for details of the courtship and wedding and even forced him to go over twice every detail of the sad accident.

"I just can't understand it," she said. "She was such a good swimmer."

"The current there is very treacherous," George repeated for the twentieth time.

The parting was the worst.

"You are my son, all I have now, and I want you always to consider this your home," she said, weeping, as she kissed him.

George was worn out when he finally got away. After all, he had not wanted to murder Edna Mae. There just was no other solution to his problem.

CHAPTER II

The French, whose outstanding characteristic is a passionate attachment to money, are perhaps the hardest-working people in the world—provided they are working for themselves. When they work for someone else, the situation changes. In the employer-employee relationship, each wants to squeeze the most out of the other. The employee tries to do as little work as possible, the employer will use any device to force the last franc's worth of effort out of each member of his staff, frequently going to the length of spending five francs to keep from losing one. Internecine warfare, endemic in any French office, is particularly virulent in one using a good deal of relatively unqualified help.

While the typing pool of any organization is rarely a stimulating place to work, that of a large insurance company in France is surely the ultimate in stupefying dullness. Assurances COPFEC was no exception. In a vast, barracklike room, with windows so grimy that even on a sunny day the world looked gray, two hundred women sat in rows of twenty before two hundred typewriters. Each wore a black nylon overall with the initials COPFEC stitched over the left breast like numbers on a convict's uniform. Every hour, the superintendent, sitting like a schoolmistress on a raised dais, keeping watchful eyes on her flock, struck a bell on her desk. Two hundred typewriters instantly ceased their clacking and their operators stood up and, stretching stiff muscles, moved around to chat. After the four minutes allowed for this dissipation, the bell was struck and, at the end of five minutes, the typing had begun again.

Ariane Quatsous, while admiring her slender white fingers listlessly hitting the keys of her typewriter at random, wished she were dead. Her machine, like the other 199, was connected to a sort of Rube Goldberg apparatus, brainchild of some dead and gone French bureaucrat, which registered the number of strokes of each typewriter in the pool of Assurances COPFEC. In this way the output of each employee could be checked. In order to keep their record up, when they had no work to do, the typists wrote over and over the saga of "Allez porter ce vieux whisky au juge blond qui fume un havane," the French equivalent of "Now is the time for all good men to come to the aid of the party."

There was no question of noiseless typewriters in this pool and their endless racket coupled with the braying of the dictaphone machines (they still used heavy black cylinders without earplugs) gave Ariane a nauseating headache. And everything was going wrong.

It had started the previous evening. Léonie Lafauve, a nurse at the Hôtel Dieu with whom Ariane shared a one-room apartment on the outskirts of Paris, had been off duty and had taken the opportunity to indulge in her favorite avocation, which was gourmet cooking. Ariane clean forgot that she was off and, noting that a movie she had missed and had wanted to see was being shown at their local cinema, had stopped in there before going home. When she got back, all hell broke loose. One of Ariane's favorite dishes was lobster quiche but, the price of lobster precluding such an extravagance, Léonie had made the quiche using, instead of lobster, the inexpensive and lowly sea snail, which has much the same consistency and flavor. She had taken the trouble to set the table properly, had bought flowers, had removed the bottle of white wine from the refrigerator to prevent it from becoming too chilled, had tossed a salad, placed a carefully selected Brie cheese and some fruit on the side table, and measured out the coffee into the pot. The quiche puffed up in the oven exactly on time. . . . And Ariane had not come home till after ten!

Léonie's recriminations about the dinner led to recollections of other past slights and injuries and it was nearly 3 A.M. before Ariane, exhausted, finally got to sleep. She woke up tired and miserably unhappy. As a final revenge, Léonie had left without waking her so that she had to hurry and, as usual in such conditions, the fates were against her. She burned her finger on the coffeepot, her shoe strap broke, she could find no stockings without runs and so had to take a pair belonging to Léonie, and she missed her usual bus and had to stand in the rain waiting for the next one. When she got within a block of her office, she heard the eight-thirty bell and joined the other latecomers in a mad dash to punch in before the ringing stopped. Middle-aged gentlemen with briefcases and the Legion of Honor in their buttonholes, fat matrons on varicose-veined legs, and the elderly, crippled by war, illness, or time, all broke into a hobbling run, passed by the young and fleet of foot. One hour's pay was deducted from the salary of those that arrived after the bell stopped ringing—half a day's pay if anyone was late twice in the same week. Ariane had been blocked at the time clock and so had been thirty seconds late punching in.

As the bleak day began, so it continued. The girls in the pool were supposed to type eight letters an hour and at quitting time each placed her output in her pigeonhole. The letters were then counted and the number entered into a register. Promotion and salary at COPFEC depended on the record maintained. Each stenographer had her "efficiency book," in which were listed her marks for punctuality, speed, conduct, accuracy, neatness, efficiency, and so forth. Every three months the supervisor called each girl to her desk and discussed her marks. Today, when Ariane's turn came, she was roundly scolded.

"Four times I have noticed you were talking when you should have been working."

"But I'd finished what I had to do."

"You had only to come to me. I would have found some work for you. Anyway, you were interfering with the work of the people you talked to. I've lowered your coefficient from B to A. That will cost you forty francs a month until your work improves. And, if it does not improve—well—we'll have to see."

When the noon bell rang Ariane, both angry and despondent, decided she could not face the well-prepared but inevitable sausage and mashed potatoes of every Thursday's lunch at the office canteen, nor the sadistic expressions of sympathy from her fellow workers, who knew, as everything in that office was known, that she had been reprimanded. She decided to get something at the corner bistro. At the bar, she took an aspirin and, not feeling hungry, followed it up with coffee and a cognac to give her a lift. Suddenly she realized this was the day the results of the national lottery were published. For years the ticket she bought every week had been Ariane's only extravagance—she could not have many on $180 a month in the world's most expensive city. She borrowed a paper from the cafe owner and, taking her ticket out of her bag, compared it with the listed winners. Suddenly she stiffened. Anxiously she compared the two numbers over and over, with rising excitement. Oh, if only it wasn't a mistake! But she seemed to have won, finally, after all these years! True, it was no fortune but, to her, $500 was an enormous sum.

She hurried to the nearest tobacconist and anxiously presented her ticket. He checked a list beside him. There was no mistake.

"You've been lucky," he smiled. "How do you want it?"

"In hundreds," she replied.

Feeling light-headed with happiness, Ariane went out into the street. Never in her whole life had she had half such a sum in her purse! Literally as well as figuratively, the clouds had dispersed, the sun was out and everything was beautiful. She forgot that she was over twenty-eight, that life seemed to offer nothing but an endless vista of work she hated, and the dreary inevitableness of an old age, with Léonie, living in the two-room village house now inhabited by the latter's mother and her sole heritage, on a small pension. Ariane herself was a foundling. At least Léonie knew who her parents were; her father had been a postman. Ariane did not even have that satisfaction.

Hearing the hated bell in the distance, Ariane instinctively began to run, then suddenly stopped short. Go back to that office this beautiful afternoon, with twenty-five hundred francs burning a hole in her handbag? No! She'd call up later to say she'd suddenly been taken—no, that wouldn't work—she would have gone to the office nurse. That her mother had been taken ill? They knew she had none. She'd say that her roommate had sprained her ankle and she had to go home to take care of her.

One thing about an office like that of COPFEC: it was pretty hard to get fired. The number of girls willing to work for starvation wages was limited. They might keep her an extra three months at coefficient A rather than B but, with her new-found wealth, what did she care? Lightheartedly she jumped on the bus that would take her to where the big shops were concentrated. Window-shopping, always one of her favorite occupations, she would find a much headier amusement with twenty-five hundred francs in her bag. She strolled from window to window and stopped in front of an elegant shoe shop. How she loathed the cheap shoes that were all she could afford! She was about to go in at least to try on a pair or two when she remembered Léonie. Anything she bought her roommate was bound to know about, living, as they did, in such proximity, and then some explanation of the purchase would have to be forthcoming. It was Léonie who managed their joint finances, putting aside every penny she could squeeze out of their combined salaries to realize her dream of opening, with Ariane, a modest restaurant somewhere in the country.

"We'd be able to get off this treadmill—to be independent. Even if we worked twice as hard, it would be for *us*," she would say as they talked over the project. "You could manage the accounts and things like that; I'll take over the kitchen. If only we had the money!"

So if she turned over her unexpected windfall to Léonie, she knew what its fate would be. But there would be advantages, too. With such a peace offering, her sin of the evening before would be more than forgiven and she would once more bask in the sunlight of Léonie's affection and approval. And Léonie, who loved to see her in becoming clothes, might even return enough for a new dress or a pair of shoes.

She owed a lot to Léonie, after all. It was Léonie who had kept her and paid for her studies at the secretarial school and who had helped her pass the necessary state professional aptitude exams; it was Léonie who, even now, contributed the lion's share to their joint expenses and who had nursed her with such loving care when she had pneumonia.

Ariane had, at sixteen, been sent by the nuns who ran the orphanage which had received her to an old people's home as a maid. The work was hard and uncongenial to a teen-ager, but as the law did not permit her to change jobs without the consent of the nuns, she had stayed there, sullen and unhappy, for two endless years. On her eighteenth birthday, freed of legal restraints, she took out of its hiding place under her mattress what money she had been able to save from an infinitesimal salary and ran away. It was on the train going to Paris that she met Léonie Lafauve. The older woman, when she learned what the situation was, insisted that Ariane come home with her, saying that a big city was no place for a pretty girl with neither money nor family. Liking the girl, Léonie persuaded her to go to school and finally found her the position with Assurances COPFEC.

In the twelve years since she left the orphanage, Ariane rarely had a chance to be with young people and never had an opportunity to acquire a beau. Occasionally men would come to visit their relatives in the old people's home but these visits were invariably hurried, and anyway, even the visitors were seldom young. At COPFEC she never had any contact with the few men who worked there who, anyway, were, for the most part, dusty or elderly or both. She had suggested once or twice that she and Léonie go to a dance hall but Léonie had been outraged; she said going on the streets would be better. That way you at least got paid.

As Ariane walked along one of the smaller streets behind the big department stores, she noticed a sign on a door which read: "Madame Solange—Marriages Arranged. Satisfaction guaranteed or your money back." She stood still, staring at the sign, her mind in a turmoil. These bureaus, she knew, were expensive and Madame Solange was one of the best-known marriage brokers in Paris. Ariane and the girls in the office had often joked about going to her, but the others, one by one, got married by more orthodox means—well, they had parents and other relatives to help them; Ariane was alone. She walked on slowly, deep in thought. Suddenly hungry, she stopped at a sidewalk cafe and ordered an omelette, a pot of tea, and—rare luxury—a package of cigarettes. She was stubbing out the fourth when she made up her mind. Paying her check, she purposely walked back to the rue de Provence, into the gloomy entry, up the dark walnut stairs and rang the doorbell of Madame Solange's office.

CHAPTER III

It was when George Zillitch had acquired enough money from his various schemes to make it worth depositing it in a Swiss bank, well out of reach of the curiosity of Internal Revenue Service agents, that he realized the fact that he had been an adopted child could be put to good use. Thus, on one of his leaves in the United States, he had flown to Chicago and had procured a copy of his birth certificate. With this he applied for a passport in the name of George Simpson and used it to enter Switzerland; it was thus in "George Simpson's" safe-deposit box in Geneva that the Altberg-Emringen jewelry was stashed away.

Before returning to Germany, after his pious mission of conveying Edna Mae's ashes to Passaic was accomplished, George took the opportunity to spend a good deal of time in the New York Public Library, poring over maps and guidebooks of South America, with a view of selecting a hideout for use till the furor which the discovery of the disappearance of the gems would be sure to raise had died down. While he did not expect that this loss would be uncovered in the immediate future, it seemed sensible not to waste time in making preparations.

Regretfully he abandoned the idea of Mexico—too many of his countrymen lived there. Brazil did not appeal to him, and Argentina seemed to be filling up with Nazis. Finally he decided on Costa Rica, which sounded like a nice little country, not too much in the public eye; its beaches were said to be superlative.

On his return to his post, his colleagues, and particularly their wives, shocked at the tragic end of his brief marriage, could not do enough to show their sympathy. When he expressed his desire to leave the scenes now so painful to him, his commanding officer arranged for his return to civilian life. A farewell party was given for him, and George, saying that he was going to the South of France for a rest before putting his nose to the grindstone again, left.

None of his colleagues ever saw him again.

In point of fact, George did his disappearing act just in time. Unknown to him, the German caretaker of the schloss, fiercely devoted to the princely House of Altberg-Emringen, which he and his ancestors had served for generations, had his own way of getting in and out of the castle, and he checked regularly on the hiding place of the jewels. Discovering the loss not long after George had left, he rushed to the commanding officer and made a formal complaint. He showed the colonel the concealed safe, now containing nothing but the empty jewel cases, and was laughed at for his pains. The colonel suggested that probably the family had taken them when they left, and when Hans Stockli indignantly denied this, suggested that the caretaker had taken them himself.

Hans then hitchhiked to Heidelberg and tried for days to see the commanding general. Here he was taken for a nut and threatened with arrest if he did not go away. On his return to the schloss he found he and his family had been evicted from the lodge they had lived in all their lives and his wife had had to return to her mother's home. Now desperate, he told his story to the local priest, who questioned him closely on it. Finally the latter promised to write to the American wife of the young prince, still a prisoner in Russia.

"But she is so far away," Hans Stockli said despondently. "And I heard she is working in a shop. What can she do?"

The priest's letter got results. Princess Rupert von Altberg-Emringen (née Kathy O'Neill) might be working at Macy's while she waited for her husband's return from captivity, but she fortunately had an uncle, Senator O'Neill, the powerful chairman of the Armed Services Committee. When he learned of his niece's loss, the fur began to fly. The newspapers took up the story eagerly: photographs of the missing gems were displayed on front pages of papers and magazines, and when, as an added bonanza, Prince Rupert von Altberg-Emringen returned from Russia at this precise moment, the press became lyrical.

The Army, meanwhile, was making gestures of desperately looking for George Zillitch to toss him to the wolves, as represented by Senator O'Neill and his committee, in an attempt to stave off the full-scale investigation the senator was proposing to launch into the extent of the plundering carried on by U. S. Army personnel in occupied territories.

When an enterprising reporter from one of the news magazines learned the story of George's ill-fated marriage and followed the trail to England and thence to Cornwall, where he dug up a witness who claimed he had seen George and Edna Mae in the sea together and then later watched while George came back alone, the press was able to add the spice of possible murder to the tasty dish they were presenting their readers. And, of course, the search for the thief and possible murderer became even more intense.

But George and the jewels seemed to have disappeared into thin air.

By circuitous means George (now Simpson) had made his way to San José, taking enough money to insure himself against want for several years while leaving most of his capital, as well as the jewelry, safely in Switzerland. What he had wanted was a comfortable life, plenty of good food, and enough of an occupation to account for his presence in Costa Rica. He was lucky. The American owner of a small bookshop specializing in English and American paperbacks suffered a heart attack. George offered to keep the place going till he recovered, but the owner preferred to go back to his home town to die, and George took over the store. The work was not onerous and it kept him supplied with reading matter at no expense to himself. He even made a little money. It was while snugly ensconced in his bookshop that George followed the story of the "disappearance of the princely heirlooms" and the search for his own person. He was particularly interested to read, when the papers began to hint at the fact that he had possibly murdered Edna Mae, that his mother-in-law stoutly insisted on his innocence both of the death of her daughter and of the theft, blaming the whole thing on a Nazi conspiracy.

The threatened investigation by Senator O'Neill did, in fact, materialize, but it yielded relatively little in the way of concrete results since, by that time, the Army had had time to close ranks and present a united front. It did, however, prove to be a boon to the senator politically, bringing him within hailing distance of the vice-presidential nomination.

Four years of self-imposed exile passed before George felt the time had come for him to begin to cash in on his unrealized wealth and start living it up. Getting in touch with Jack Venturian, he arranged to meet him in Geneva. It took the fence the best part of ten days to examine the jewels.

"It'll take me a good deal of time to get rid of the stones in settings. We'd better start with the loose stones."

Jack Venturian spent three years dispersing the gems; after he had taken the lion's share, George was the happy possessor of two million dollars, which his Swiss bank invested for him.

George, by now in his mid-forties, settled down to a life of leisure and comfort on the Côte d'Azur. Knowing he was still being sought by Interpol and too shrewd to make the mistake of throwing money around in a way that might attract attention to himself, he bought a modest apartment in Cannes, furnished it with antiques he acquired in the auction rooms of Monte Carlo (and realized how *very well* he and Edna Mae had done by the various Army wives they had supplied; the prices he had to pay were quadruple what they had received for their bibelots), and joined a sporting club. His only real luxury was to hire a first-rate cook. But when his apartment was finally arranged to his taste, which, over the years, had become excellent, the days began to have a horrid sameness; the other club members, the only people he knew, bored him (and, it had to be admitted, he bored them), and, while he quite enjoyed a mild flutter at the tables from time to time, he was no gambler, just as he was no drinker. The life of leisure and plenty he had so looked forward to began to pall; he suddenly detested the Côte d'Azur and all its denizens. He was sick of food from the sea, particularly bouillabaisse, and of things cooked in oil with tomatoes, green peppers, or eggplant, and he was tired to death of the climate where the only change from sunshine and blue skies was hot winds and cold drizzle, particularly depressing because there was so little heating indoors.

He decided to go to Paris.

* * *

It took George five years to get as tired of Paris as he had been of Cannes. The process was delayed by his taking a flier in the business world. Through an ad in the Paris edition of the *Herald Tribune,* he got in touch with a man seeking capital to launch a new product. When George learned that this was an inflatable, life-size plastic doll, [equipped with the usual female physical adjuncts] he decided to invest a few thousand dollars. The dolls —redheads, blondes, white, yellow, black—were advertised chiefly in theatrical publications and proved to be an instant success. George had netted a quarter of a million dollars when he felt the time had come to sell out, keeping a few specimens as souvenirs. The dolls were unpatentable and, as he had foreseen, imitators flooded the market. His partner, less farsighted, lost his shirt.

But, after this excursion into the business world, ennui once more set in. George was lonely.

Wanting to be in the center of Paris, George had bought himself a pleasant apartment in the Cité Rétiro, an elegant little alley that ran from the Faubourg St. Honoré to the place de la Madeleine. There he and his cat frequently sat at a window and watched the busy life below them. An assistant to the chef of the well-known restaurant across from his apartment prepared lunch in George's own kitchen before going on duty. For his dinner, George either went to a restaurant or fixed something himself, and a daily woman took care of the place. For his intimate needs, George patronized from time to time, a very satisfactory though expensive "house" off the avenue Kléber.

Most afternoons between 4:30 and 7 P.M. George Simpson sat at an outside table at the Café de la Paix, watching the crowds go by, hoping some compatriot would sit down at a table near enough for him to be able to begin to talk to him. Since the American Express was just around the corner and the Café de la Paix was almost as much a sight-seeing must as the Louvre, flies quite frequently walked into George's carefully spun web. While these improvised acquaintanceships frequently could be extended through the evening, they rarely lasted much longer. For the most part, the people he picked up were passing through Paris, not residents. But there was another reason for the brevity of these friendships. Never a particularly entertaining companion, George had become, at fifty, one of the world's prize bores—moreover, a bore who did not even drink.

On a warm September afternoon, George had had no luck in picking up a stray English-speaking tourist in spite of his prominently displayed *Herald Tribune.* He had on his "autumn clothes." Overweight was still his major problem in life. Since good food had practically become George's raison d'être, in order to be able to continue gourmet eating without becoming monstrously obese, he spent two to three months of every year undergoing the cure at either Vittel or Baden-Baden, sometimes going for one month to each. (Once, at Baden-Baden, the Prince von Altberg-Emringen and his American wife had been pointed out to him. Since they were in a chauffeur-driven Rolls, he decided their fortunes had survived the loss he had inflicted.)

George was therefore forced to have two sets of clothes: those he wore for a couple of months or so after his return, forty pounds lighter, from his cure and those he wore as the inches began to gain on him again.

Paying for his orangeade and the pastries he had eaten, George went off toward the Printemps to buy a gadget to pit olives and cherries which he had seen advertised. Having completed his purchase, he went out the back door and found himself in the rue de Provence, which ran behind the department store. It was the first time he had been on this rather dismal street, a fashionable one of Paris up to the turn of the century, and he looked at what had been elegant apartment houses, now mostly turned into offices, with a certain interest. From time to time, George caught a glimpse of the decorative plaster molding for which the French were famous and, in one place, of a charming painted ceiling. Glancing at the various name plates at the entrance, one in particular caught his eye: "Madame Solange— Agence Matrimoniale." He stopped and stared. Why not, after all? A wife to see to his comforts, to share his bed and his life! Why had he not thought of it earlier? The American women he had picked up, either alone, in pairs (he never spoke to them if there were more than two together), or with their husbands, had appalled him. They seemed to have no doubt whatsoever of their own worth, of the indisputable validity of their points of view, of their right to make all decisions. George shuddered at the thought. What he wanted was a nice, pretty, docile French wife, not too young.

Slowly he walked on and spent the next two days deep in reflection. On the third day, he purposefully returned to the rue de Provence and walked into Madame Solange's parlor.

CHAPTER IV

After leaving Madame Solange's office, Ariane went home, almost sick with excitement and emotion. The marriage broker had been very optimistic about the possibility of finding a suitable husband for Ariane, whose exceptional prettiness and dainty figure she had highly approved. She was just the right age, too. Not too old and not too young.

"It is, of course, a pity that there is no possibility of a dowry or even, ultimately, of an inheritance," Madame Solange said. "However, a stable job with a reliable firm is considered, by many men, a most satisfactory substitute. Tell me, do you have furniture, linen, silver, or something of that nature to contribute to the house?"

Ariane shook her head.

"All that belongs to my roommate."

Madame Solange glanced sharply at the girl.

"Have you told your roommate about your plan to visit me?"

"I didn't know myself until I saw the sign on the door. It all came about because I won the money in the lottery. I wouldn't have been able to afford to come to see you if that hadn't happened."

"Will it be all right if I address my communications to you at home?"

Ariane looked startled.

"Oh, no! You mustn't do that. I wouldn't want to tell Léonie unless . . . unless there was something definite and I was really going to get married."

"How can I get in touch with you, then?"

"The man who runs the cafe near my office I know frequently

takes in the mail of some of the girls in my office. They pay him a little."

"Very well. Give me the address. You'll hear from me in about ten days. Don't worry. We'll find you a nice husband. Just trust Madame Solange."

Ariane scribbled the address down, paid the fifty-franc fee, and left the office, feeling almost light-headed. Léonie, thank goodness, was on night duty this week and would have left the apartment before Ariane returned. This would give her time to compose herself and plan how to keep the meetings Madame Solange had said she would arrange a secret from her room-mate. To ease her feeling of guilt, she put a thousand francs in an envelope, with an affectionate note, and laid it on Léonie's pillow.

When the girl had gone, Madame Solange moved an index-card box toward her and began checking the names in it. Suddenly she stopped. That American who had come in two days before! He'd be the very thing. Opening a drawer of her desk, she riffled through several folders until she found the right one. Carefully she read through it. Why, Ariane Quatsous exactly answered the description of his requirements! There was a considerable difference in age, of course, but Ariane was nearly thirty, and twenty years was not an excessive gap. Pushing the file away from her, Madame Solange picked up the telephone and dialed George Simpson's number.

*   *   *

All morning, on the Saturday he was to make the acquaintance of the girl Madame Solange had selected for him as a possible wife, George was torn between a desire to cancel the whole project and a sense of excitement and adventure that had been woefully lacking in his life the past few years. Several times he reached for the phone to call Madame Solange and each time he withdrew it. Just meeting the young woman, he finally decided, would not commit him to anything except lunch. Besides, she might not like him.

George, while telling Madame Solange that he was more than

comfortably off and was not looking for any pecuniary contribution from his wife, refrained from telling her how much money he actually had.

It took him some time to decide on a suitable restaurant in which to meet, and he finally picked on the uptown Prunier. It was pretty good, and anyway, he felt like some lobster. Arranging to meet Ariane at one fifteen, he arrived a quarter of an hour early and told the headwaiter he was expecting a guest. Then he sat down at a secluded corner table from which he could watch the door and awaited the arrival of his prospective wife.

* * *

The difficulty, Ariane found, of living in great intimacy with anyone was that it was next to impossible to have any secrets. Léonie had wept with pleasure over Ariane's gift of her lottery winnings and had done everything possible to express her gratitude and affection. When Madame Solange finally notified her of the date, hour, and place of her meeting with the wealthy American who was seeking a wife, Ariane found it impossible to behave normally, and her manner was so strange Léonie feared she was sickening for something and insisted on taking her temperature.

With some of the money she had withheld from her winnings, Ariane bought a well-made navy blue outfit from a shop that specialized in actresses' discards. Here she also was able to pick up a respectable handbag at a moderate price. Shoes and gloves she bought new, and she also bought some underwear. She had no intention of permitting Mr. Simpson to sample the wares he was proposing to buy, at least not at this stage of the game, but she felt it was best to be on the safe side.

Since she could not take her purchases home with her, the question was what to do? Finally she bought a cheap suitcase, packed it, and left it at the railroad station. Saturday morning she would have her hair done, and change into her new clothes.

The meeting went off very well. George's spirit soared when he saw the slender, well-formed young woman, escorted by the headwaiter, advancing toward his table. Her large round blue

eyes, with their dark lashes, were set in a dimpled oval face and
surmounted by short black curls. She was neatly, even smartly
dressed; George could hardly believe his luck as he stood up to
greet her.

During the early part of the luncheon, conversation between
these two prospective life mates was inclined to be jerky, but over
the excellent champagne George had ordered as an apéritif,
Ariane began to relax a little and to look about her with interest,
glancing shyly from time to time at her companion.

Madame Solange had told her Mr. Simpson was inclined to be
corpulent and Ariane could but agree with this description. On
the other hand, he was not flabby, and if his eyes were protuber-
ant and his mouth too full, at least he was not yet bald and his
face, on the whole, was not unpleasing. He seemed kind. And as
the caviar he had ordered, a delicacy which she had never before tasted, was followed by a large lobster in a champagne
sauce, Ariane's spirits rose and she began to look about her at
the other guests, particularly noting that the other women were,
on the whole, no better dressed than she was. This discovery
made her feel surer of herself and she smiled at George. She
had, so far, confined herself to monosyllabic answers to his questions; now, she began to venture a few remarks.

One difficulty was that despite the years he had lived in
France, George's French, while adequate for day-to-day living,
was not really of conversation caliber. However, he seemed to
understand everything she said, though she was more or less
forced to guess at what he was saying. About food, though,
George could be fluent.

"Do you like these côtes de veau?" he asked as the stuffed veal
chops, covered with a rich tarragon sauce followed the lobster.
Ariane tasted hers.

"Very good," she approved, "but I like the way Léonie does
them better. She nearly always serves them cold. Instead of
pâté de foie gras, which is both expensive and heavy, she uses
a ham mousse for the stuffing. In the summer, after the chops
are cooked, she sets them in aspic. Sometimes she mixes the

pâté in the stuffing with toasted bread crumbs and after the chops are cooked dips them in a chaud-froid sauce."

George stared at the girl, surprised at her sudden loquacity.

"You know a good deal about cooking," he finally said.

Ariane laughed.

"I should," she said. "Cooking is Léonie's hobby—no, her passion."

"Who is Léonie?" George asked.

"My roommate. We've been sharing an apartment for years so, naturally, I've learned a good deal about food. *I* can't cook, though; Léonie will never let me."

"Does your friend run a restaurant?"

"She wishes she did. That's her great dream! But it takes capital to start something like that in France. She'd be marvelous! There's *nothing* she can't make, even in our little kitchen, which is not like a restaurant kitchen. Do you know, she even made an eel pâté one Christmas? She had read that it was a speciality of one of the big Paris restaurants and that it was very difficult to make. It took her three days and was very expensive, but I've never tasted anything like it! She wants to try to make it some time using carp roe, but I don't believe it would improve it. I'm sure her eel pâté was better than the one the restaurant is so famous for."

"What does your friend do?"

"She's a nurse at the Hôtel Dieu."

"I'd like to meet her," George said. But this innocuous remark had the effect of suddenly silencing Ariane.

It was after three o'clock when they finished their coffee and George called for the bill.

"Can I see you tomorrow?" he asked suddenly as they went out the door.

Ariane shook her head.

"Tomorrow is Léonie's one Sunday off in the month," she said. "I don't like to leave her."

"Perhaps I could come to see you?"

"Oh no!" Ariane exclaimed, turning pale. "Not . . . not now.

You see, I haven't told Léonie . . . I mean . . . about Madame Solange."

George was silent as they walked along the avenue Victor Hugo toward a taxi stand. Suddenly he stopped.

"I want to see you again very much—and soon. Do you like me enough to see me again, to decide whether you can like me more?"

Ariane nodded. Really, she thought, he's not bad-looking at all standing . . . he's much taller than I realized, and you hardly notice his double chin.

"When, then? Perhaps Monday."

"Well, of course, I work all day."

"Monday evening?"

"Can I let you know? It depends on Léonie's schedule."

"May I call you?"

"We have no phone at home and we're not allowed to get calls at the office unless it's a matter of life and death."

"Here's my number. Promise you'll call me?"

"I promise."

"That's a good girl," and George gave Ariane's arm an approving squeeze. "Now where can I take you?"

"Nowhere. I have shopping to do and then I'll catch a train home."

"Are you sure?"

"Yes, really."

George leaned over and kissed Ariane gently on her forehead. "Goodbye, beautiful. I'll be dreaming about you."

Ariane was in a pensive mood as she got in the Métro to go to the station. She had not found the touch of George Simpson's lips disagreeable. At the station, she changed back into her everyday clothes, neatly packing away her new things and hoping they would not get too wrinkled.

When Ariane got home, she found a note from Léonie telling her she had had to leave suddenly for Lille; her mother had had a stroke and was dying.

"I hate to leave you alone, my very dear, and will come back as soon as I can. You know where to write to me."

Ariane sank into a chair, stunned. What an extraordinary piece of good luck! It was almost an omen—an indication from on high that this was meant.

Jumping to her feet she rushed down the stairs and out to the nearest pay telephone and dialed George Simpson's number.

* * *

CHAPTER V

During the following week, Ariane was out with George every evening. On Friday, he wanted to take her to Maxim's.

"I can't," she said regretfully. "I read that Friday is the 'dress' night at Maxim's and I don't have anything suitable to wear."

"We can soon fix that," George replied. "I'll take you shopping."

"I can't let you do that!"

"Why not? We'll soon be married." George paused. "Won't we?" he finally added.

Ariane silently nodded several times.

"In that case, we'll go shopping tomorrow morning."

"I can't. My office—"

"Call them up and tell them you've quit."

Ariane looked frightened.

"Oh, I couldn't do that!" she exclaimed. "It would be a black mark against me the next time I look for work."

"You'll not be looking for work, young lady. You just told me you would marry me, remember?"

Ariane looked unconvinced.

"I'll call up to say I'm not well. They don't insist on a doctor's certificate for just one day," she compromised.

The next day was the happiest in Ariane's life. George brushed aside her suggestion of department stores and, instead, took her to the boutiques of what was left of France's great dressmaking houses. They finally selected a full-skirted sapphire-blue velvet dress with a low-cut satin top of the same shade that set off Ariane's tiny waist to perfection. A matching velvet bolero, lined and piped with the satin, made the dress a versatile one.

Gold gloves, bag, and shoes completed the ensemble, and George looked proudly at his future bride.

"You'll knock 'em for a loop," he said in English. "And now let's go buy a ring," he added in French.

In the jewelry shop on the place Vendôme to which he took her, George was pensive as he learned the prices of quite modest rings and regretted he had not saved at least one of the loose stones he had acquired at the Schloss Altberg. "Talk of thieves!" he reflected. Here they were asking one hundred times the price at which he had sold his stones for gems nothing like as good.

George had wanted to give Ariane a sapphire to match her eyes, but, while she said nothing, he sensed that to her a diamond was the only suitable stone for an engagement ring.

Suddenly he remembered that the marquise diamond ring and the pearl necklace he had given Edna Mae at the time of their engagement had not been sold with the rest of the Altberg-Emringen jewels and was, in fact, in his apartment. None of the rings he and Ariane had been shown was half as impressive; it seemed a pity not to use it. Also, the creamy smoothness of the pearls, he thought with satisfaction, would enhance Ariane's delicate beauty. George swept her out of the shop, promising her a pleasant surprise later on.

Ariane wept with gratitude and pleasure when, before they left for Maxim's, George slipped the ring on her finger and fastened the pearls around her neck, resolutely refusing to recall the previous time he had done just this for another woman.

The dinner that night was eminently successful and Ariane had the time of her life. A fervent reader of *Ici Paris* and *France Dimanche,* two publications devoted to keeping an unwavering eye on public figures, particularly in the entertainment world, Ariane was able to point out several celebrities at neighboring tables. She felt the world had nothing more to offer her when on the stroke of midnight, Aristotle Onassis arrived with a party and was seated at the table next to theirs.

It was late when they left the restaurant and the only form of transportation available were taxis; George put Ariane into one of them and paid the driver. He wanted to accompany her home but she would not hear of this.

It was 3 A.M. when she finally reached the dreary cement cube which, with hundreds of thousands of similar cubes, constituted France's contribution to twentieth-century architectural art, a contribution that made one long for some selective natural catastrophe.

As Ariane got out her key, she noticed, to her horror, a line of light under the door. For a time she stood paralyzed, her mind racing. She wanted desperately to run away, back to the taxi, but it had long since gone. Suddenly the door was flung open and Léonie stood facing her. Her mouth fell open when she saw the elegant young woman at the door. The two stared at each other.

"How is your mother?" Ariane finally faltered, trying to make her way past her roommate into the apartment.

"Where have you been?" Léonie asked, letting her in and shutting the door. In the better light, she was able to take in the clothes, the ring, the necklace. "Where have you been?" she repeated, her question on a higher note.

When there was still no answer, Léonie slapped Ariane hard across the cheek.

"So!" she said between clenched teeth, slapping the other cheek. "As soon as I'm out of the way, you take to the streets! So that's what you've been all this time—a tart!"

"No, no!" Ariane cried out, cringing under the blows. "Please, please! I'm not a tart. I'll tell you all about it! Just listen, please, Léonie."

"Where did you get those clothes?" Léonie screamed. "I suppose your pimp dolled you up like that. Was it he who gave you the money you told me you won in the lottery?"

"Just listen, Léonie," Ariane sobbed, tears pouring down her reddened cheeks. "I'm going to get married!"

Léonie was suddenly very still and stared at Ariane, her eyes blazing in her white face.

"Married!" she repeated. "I don't believe you! You don't know anybody to marry!"

"I do. I do! I'm going to marry an American."

Léonie's eyes narrowed.

"How long has this been going on under my nose?"

"Léonie, please sit down and let me tell you about it."

The older woman sank into the armchair and Ariane knelt down on the floor by her side and began to talk while Léonie listened in silence, her face expressionless.

Somehow, the fact that Ariane had met the man she knew as George Simpson through a matrimonial agency rather than as a result of mutual attraction seemed to give Léonie some satisfaction.

"So you've had enough of your old Léonie!" she finally said bitterly. "After all she has done for you!"

"Léonie, it's just that I can't face going through life in that *horrible* office. Day after day after day!"

"*I* work day after day after day," Léonie pointed out.

"I know. And you work much harder than I do. But you can feel you are needed—that your work benefits people—that it is at least interesting. Mine destroys the soul! I'd a thousand times rather die than go through life like that," and Ariane began to sob, her head in Léonie's lap.

Almost involuntarily, Léonie's hand began to stroke the dark curls. She gave a heavy sigh.

"Well, if you must go, you must. I can't force you to stay with me. I shall be lonely, Ariane, a lonely old woman."

"Léonie, you won't be lonely. I won't let you be!"

"You'll have other interests—and a husband to love."

"Love!" Ariane sat up. "You don't think I *love* George?"

"Why shouldn't I think so? Marriage and love go hand in hand. At least, so I've always been told."

Ariane got up and stood before the mirror, smoothing her dress.

"A little discomfort from time to time is a small price to pay for—this," she replied, her voice hard. "To pay for things for both of us."

CHAPTER VI

The French government, in its wisdom, frowns on marriages on a whim; it insists that its citizens have plenty of time for reflection and makes them jump through a good many hoops on their way to the altar, or, rather, to the mayor's office. This is particularly true in the case of a French person intending to marry a foreigner.

The period that followed her engagement was exhausting for Ariane, and if her hatred of the treadmill from which she had so recently liberated herself had been less violent she might not have been able to withstand Léonie's tactics, which alternated cajolements and reproaches, pleadings and threats of suicide, thin-lipped silence and torrents of abuse.

Torn by the feeling that she owed a debt of gratitude both to her old friend and to her generous fiancé, she cast about desperately for some way of reconciling the two. Ariane and George were sitting over their coffee in a country inn on the outskirts of Paris one day, discussing their future, when George made a remark that gave Ariane a glimmer of an idea as to how this might be accomplished.

"It wouldn't take much to turn this place into a real money-maker," he commented, looking around the room at the empty tables. "Just a first-rate kitchen and better service. I used to be in the hotel business, you know, and I've often thought I'd like to run a little place of my own."

Ariane had not known; George rarely talked about his past. Now she was silent as they drove back to Paris, mulling over an idea that had come to her.

"Well, I don't see why we shouldn't," she finally said as she got out of the car in front of George's apartment.

"Shouldn't what?" George asked.

"Have a little hotel." But George drove off to a garage to park the car and Ariane's remark had been forgotten when he rejoined her. It was nearly midnight when Ariane finally left.

"Why don't you spend the night?" George asked as he watched her dress. They had been lovers for nearly two weeks and Ariane, who had rather dreaded the ultimate intimacy, was surprised to find it not as distasteful as she had expected, in spite of the fact that George was hardly the answer to a maiden's dream.

"Léonie is off duty tomorrow. I really must go back this evening."

"Say, when am I going to meet this roommate of yours?"

"Well, she works very hard and is tired when she gets home," Ariane replied, running a comb through her hair. "And, of course, she's upset about our getting married. She's quite alone in the world. But I'm sure, once we're married, she will get used to the idea."

Ariane stooped down and kissed George goodbye.

"Be sure to take a cab," he said. "Have you got enough money?"

She nodded and, with a wave of her hand, hurried out the door.

As the taxi drew up in front of her home, she glanced up at the window and saw the light was on. As she had expected, Léonie was home.

Her roommate, Ariane noted as she entered the little apartment, had been crying.

"Oh, Léonie, please!" Sitting down on the arm of the chair, she put her arm around her friend.

"I can't help it! I can't help it!" the older woman sobbed. "I'm going to be so lonely."

"You won't be lonely if you come to live with us!" Ariane exclaimed triumphantly.

"Live with you? Are you mad?" Léonie exclaimed, interrupting her sobs. "Do you think for one minute—"

"Listen to me, Léonie. I've had an idea. Hasn't your dream always been to have a restaurant?"

Léonie shrugged.

"It *was*," she answered, drying her eyes. "But that was when I thought that you and I—"

"It's going to be 'you and I'—you and I and George. Because it's been George's dream, too. He can open a hotel and you'll run it."

"Me? Accept favors from *your* husband? I'd rather die!"

"Oh, Lélé, you're just trying to be difficult. I told you, it's not 'favors.' George has plenty of money and nothing to do. His one interest in life is food and he knows almost as much about it as you do. Do you realize that he spent a whole *year* going to every restaurant that has even one star in the Michelin guidebook? Also, he told me just this evening that he used to be in the hotel business. So all three of us can work to make a little hotel George will open a success. We will work together. You would take over the kitchen, George would run the place and I could do the bookkeeping and reservations and things like that."

"Ariane!" Léonie scoffed. "Those are pipe dreams!"

"They can be made to come true! I tell you, George is rich!"

"How do you know he's so rich?" Léonie asked suspiciously.

"Madame Solange told me she was satisfied with the proofs he presented."

"And why should a rich man have to go to a marriage broker for a wife?"

This was a question that Ariane had asked herself more than once.

"He's a foreigner here. He has no friends and there is no way for him to meet people."

"Why has a rich man no friends? If he's lonely, why does he live in a foreign country? Why doesn't he go back to his own?"

"I don't know," Ariane answered doubtfully. "He *says* he lives here because of the food. Lélé—*please* just do this one thing! Let me bring George to dinner. I *do* believe in you, and after he's had one of your meals, I think *he's* going to be the one to push the idea of a hotel."

It took Ariane a long time to talk her friend into agreeing to invite George to a meal, and dawn was breaking when the two women finally got to bed and fell into an exhausted sleep.

The next morning, Léonie was white-faced and withdrawn, but seemed to accept the fact that she was to meet her friend's future husband.

"I'm so anxious for you to know him!" Ariane said. "When can I ask him to dinner?"

"Give me a little time. I can't bear to think of meeting the man who is going to take you away from me."

"But we've been through all that. He's not going to take me without you. I want us all three to be together. That's why I'm so anxious for him to come to dinner here."

"My poor child, that sort of project never works out."

Ariane started to exclaim that in that case she would not get married at all but suddenly broke off. Léonie noted the abruptly ended sentence and sighed deeply.

"All right, then. Bring him—let's see—next Thursday, if he wants to come. That will be my next day off."

It took all Léonie's powers of dissimulation to present an appearance of acceptance of Ariane's marriage, and she only half heard the young woman's light-hearted chatter as she talked about her wedding plans. Léonie still intended to fight, but until she met her enemy she could not know what weapons would be the most effective. She began to look forward to the meeting.

Léonie was not French for nothing and, while she thought it was improbable, it was at least possible that Ariane might be able to persuade her husband to provide financial backing for a restaurant venture even if the hotel project came to nothing. It would be foolish to cut off her nose to spite her face. If she really was going to lose Ariane, she might as well salvage what she could. So the meal, she decided, would be as good as she could make it.

The day before the dinner, Léonie went to market and, checking on what was at its best, planned her menu with care. And on Thursday she started her dinner first thing in the morning. She was a neat, deft cook and her kitchen, as she completed each step, was as tidy as when she went into it.

By five o'clock, the stuffed breast of veal was slowly roasting, the gâteau Isabelle was in the refrigerator, the hard-boiled eggs and garlic croutons were beside the spinach, which had only to be reheated. Quickly she rolled out strips of pastry and laid them, lattice fashion, across the open-face potato pie, taking out of the refrigerator the cream that was to be added once the pie was in the oven. Then she made four dozen small thin pancakes, rolling them around a stuffing of chicken liver purée into the shape of tiny cigars. These had still to be dipped in beaten egg and bread crumbs and quickly fried in deep fat, but this she would do after her guest had arrived, as these appetizers had to be served hot.

Yes, everything seemed ready. Léonie went into their living room, set the table, and looked around her. It was a dreary place, with ugly furniture; the sofa, which converted into a double bed at night, looked as hard and uncomfortable to sit in as it was. But the little apartment was as clean and tidy as human hands could make it; the curtains were starched, the waxed linoleum on the floor gleamed, and the woodwork was a brilliant white. Then she took a leisurely bath and was reading the paper when Ariane and George arrived, the latter red-faced and panting from the exertion of the long climb up to the fifth floor.

"This is George, Léonie," the younger woman said. "George, this is my friend, Léonie Lafauve."

"I feel I already know you, Ariane has talked so much about you," George said, still panting a little as he shook hands.

Léonie's beady eyes quickly took in every detail of her guest's appearance: his thinning reddish hair streaked with gray, his too-protuberant eyes, his double chin, and the girth which, she deduced from a telltale ridge under his trousers, he attempted to disguise by the use of a rubber corset—all gave her sardonic satisfaction.

For his part, George found it hard to account for Ariane's devotion to the square-built woman with a fairly luxuriant mustache and pepper-and-salt hair worn in a crew cut.

"There is some champagne in the refrigerator, Ariane," Léonie said. "Pour it out while I put something in the oven." A few minutes later she was back with the appetizers.

"I hope these will keep you busy till dinner is ready," she said and picked up the glass of champagne Ariane had poured out for her. "To a long and happy marriage," she added as she raised her glass. Then she returned to the kitchen. It was nearly half an hour before Léonie came back into the room with the eggplant-and-shrimp soufflé. She was interested to note that the great pile of rich stuffed pancakes had melted to one solitary broken one.

While George made some effort at the beginning of the meal to engage his two hostesses in conversation, as perfection followed perfection he ceased to take any interest in anything beyond what was on his plate.

He accepted three helpings of the breast of veal, crusty outside, fork-tender inside. The smoked ham with which she had lined the pocket gave a distinctive flavor both to the meat and to the light mushroom, onion, and bread stuffing which had been liberally mixed with truffled liver pâté. There was not a crumb left of the large potato pie, the pastry of which lay on the tongue like a snowflake.

"What did you do to this spinach? I've never tasted anything like it," George was sufficiently roused to ask as he helped himself liberally a second time.

"That is my secret. However, as this is a special occasion, I'll confide it to you. Nothing could be simpler. I cooked it five days ago. Then, every day, I put it back on the fire with a new dressing of butter. Thus, when you finally serve it, it has much the same consistency as purée, but I like it much better."

"And the dressing in this salad? It doesn't seem to be any kind of vinegar I can recognize."

"That's an experiment I made and I flatter myself it is successful. I use pomegranate juice instead of vinegar. As a matter of fact, I also marinate cubed mutton in pomegranate juice when I make shish kebab."

"Pomegranate juice! I'd never have thought of that!"

The gâteau Isabelle, which ended the meal, was rich but not cloying.

"*Vous êtes une fourchette intrépide*, Mr. Simpson," Léonie

commented, putting the last of the almond and chocolate dessert on his plate.

"I have eaten far too much, but it's the best meal I've ever had!" George declared as he loosened his belt. "Ariane is right. You're a genius. I hope you've taught her some of your secrets."

"As a cook I'm hopeless," Ariane said. "But, of course, compared to Léonie, almost anybody is."

"I'm surprised you're not working in one of the big restaurants," George said. "I should think you could make a fortune."

"I don't have the qualifications. In France, to be a professional cook, you have either to go to a hotel school or, even better, you must work for years as an apprentice under a great chef. I have taught myself. The only way I could make a profession of cooking would be to open my own restaurant, and, alas, I don't have the means." And Léonie, picking up a tray, took the soiled dishes out of the room while Ariane cleared off the table, folded it, restored it to its position against the wall, and then brought in the coffee and some liqueurs.

When, a little later, Léonie returned, George was pensively sipping Kirschwasser. Finally, he put his glass down.

"*I* have money," he said. "Why don't we open a small hotel—all three of us? You, of course, would be in charge of the restaurant."

It was as simple as that.

* * *

At first Léonie seemed not particularly interested in the plans Ariane and George discussed but, as their feasibility became more and more apparent, even she began to join in the conversation and, when George brought his Michelin guide up from the car, all three of them pored over the maps showing the whereabouts of the various starred restaurants and hotels of France.

"We might as well forget about anything between Paris and the Côte d'Azur. That area is already overcrowded with first-rate restaurants," George said. "And in Alsace, *all* the restaurants are good, so that is out."

"According to this map, the north doesn't seem to have any-thing much in the restaurant line. Between Paris and Lille seems to be a gastronomic desert," Ariane remarked.

"And with reason. It's depressing country, the climate is bad, and the people dour," Léonie replied. "I know. I come from near Lille. What we want is to be near one or two prosperous but rather dull towns so that our permanent clients will more or less be locals. Tourists are profitable during the season, but it's the locals that keep a place making money all the year round."

It was nearly 3 A.M. when it was decided that, on their honey-moon, George and Ariane would scout around looking for an ideal location. Two regions seemed particularly hopeful: that between Limoges and Poitiers, wealthy towns both and cer-tainly dull, and the region around Brest in Brittany.

After that, the days flew by. Léonie, bearing in mind the projected venture, began to take an interest in the wedding and bought Ariane an elegant fitted dressing case which made a con-siderable hole in her hard-earned savings. Ariane's gratitude knew no bounds.

"But, really, you shouldn't have, Léonie," she said, with tears in her eyes.

"I want you to have something to remember your old Léonie by," her friend said.

In what seemed like no time at all, Ariane found herself stand-ing beside George while the local mayor, resplendent in his sash of office, pronounced them man and wife.

After a copious wedding luncheon provided by Léonie, George and Ariane left on their honeymoon, headed for Montoir-sur-le-Loir, which boasted a two-star restaurant which George had unaccountably missed on previous trips through the Châteaux region. On the days that followed, Ariane realized that George was planning their trip for reasons more of gastronomy than of house-hunting. The farther they got from Paris, the more in-terested he was in the former and less in the latter. It was only through Ariane's prodding that they visited notaires and real estate brokers, but what they saw was either very expensive or very dull, and George's interest in the whole project seemed to lapse. This, Ariane thought, was due more to her husband's laziness and boredom with the mechanics of finding a place than to objections to the project. So it was Ariane who found a short cut in their search. As she was waiting in the lobby of the hotel while George paid the bill, she leafed through a booklet entitled *Chefs-d'oeuvre en Péril,* which listed châteaux, convents, priories, and other historic buildings which had been abandoned, sometimes for centuries, and which could be purchased for a nominal sum provided the new owner would undertake their restoration. In certain cases and under certain conditions, the government would even give financial assistance to anyone seriously undertaking such a restoration. Ariane turned the pages of the booklet with rising excitement and when George joined her she showed him the picture of an abandoned monastery in Brittany, right on the sea. One wing seemed to have fallen in but, for the most part, according to the photograph, it was beautiful, quite large, and in relatively good shape. Even George was interested and agreed to drive there at once.

If anything, from an architectural point of view, the place was even lovelier than Ariane had expected it to be. However, she was somewhat dismayed by the condition of the interior—more so than George was.

"It will take money, of course," he said, surveying the dilapidations caused by time, neglect, and the weather. "But it is easier to install heating, electricity, plumbing, and so forth in a place that has never had them than to tear out what is already there in order to modernize. It's a good site and there are plenty of grounds . . . if you really want to undertake something like this, I can swing it."

Ariane had no doubts about that and they contacted the owners of the ruin to make them an offer. It took several weeks for the purchase to go through. Ariane was surprised and grateful when George insisted that the deed be registered in her name.

"How long do you think it will be before the place is ready?" Ariane asked her husband anxiously.

George shrugged.

"It's hard to tell . . . it depends a good deal on how lucky we are in finding workmen. At least six months—probably nearer nine."

"Oh, dear. That's a long time. Poor Léonie. I must tell her."

"I hope you're sure she isn't going to back out?" George said. "Because it is her cooking that will make or break this venture."

"Oh, no. I'm sure she will come. Why, it's what she has always wanted! Now I must write to her. She'll be so happy!"

Léonie received Ariane's letter when she returned from the hospital the following day. She read it through several times and gave no outward signs of any particular happiness. After a light supper, she sat down under a lamp, read the letter once more, then sat staring into space for over an hour. Finally, her mind made up, she took a bath and went to bed.

CHAPTER VII

Ken McCabe had plenty of time for reflection as he lay in the American Hospital in Neuilly waiting for his body to recover from the effects of three bullet holes, two of which had required long and delicate surgery. He was the first casualty suffered by the Paris office of the United States Bureau of Narcotics, and his shooting had been something of an accident.

He and a French colleague had been apartment hunting at the same time, and Jean Labruyère found a very attractive place which was well beyond his means. Since the perpetual housing shortage in Paris makes it imperative to come to an immediate decision in such a case since a line of tired searchers is invariably waiting eagerly to snap up any trove at a prospective tenant's slightest pause for reflection, Labruyère took the apartment and then talked the American into sharing it with him, pointing out that, besides living comfortably and reasonably, there would be the added advantage of each becoming more fluent in the other's tongue. The arrangement had worked well for four years; Ken spoke French better than any of his American colleagues and Jean's English became more and more Americanized.

While their work was in the same field and they constantly met at office conferences, the two men had never actually worked together on a specific case. Then one evening Jean Labruyère, who had a remarkable memory for faces, had stopped for a drink in a large cafe on the Place des Ternes, not far from the apartment, and noticed that the bartender had on dark glasses. Dark glasses at any time attracted Labruyère's attention; those worn late in the evening aroused all his interest. As he sipped his drink, he examined the man carefully. Disregarding the color of his hair, of his mustache and small beard, he unobtrusively concentrated his attention on the distance between the bartender's eyes, the shape of his head, the position of his ears, and the distance between his nose and chin. He finally paid his bill and left, feeling troubled. He was unable to put a name to the combination of features, but there was something familiar there. It was while he and Ken were having coffee after a leisurely dinner that Jean suddenly put his cup down.

"It was Jo-Jo!" he exclaimed.

Ken McCabe looked confused.

"Who was Jo-Jo?" he asked.

"The barman I told you looked familiar. We caught him at the Gare de Lyon three years ago transporting twenty kilos of heroin in his valise. He got ten years but escaped from prison last year." The Frenchman glanced at his watch. "That cafe closes at eleven o'clock and he'll probably go off duty then. I'm going down there."

"It'll be better if there are two of us. I'll come with you."

"Well, you're not really supposed—"

"Oh, I know that. It can all be a coincidence, if anything comes of it. You happened to be with me in my car when you spotted this guy on his way home and we followed him."

The two men sat outside the cafe in Ken's car and watched as tables and chairs were brought in from the terrace and stacked and the lights were gradually extinguished.

"There he is," Jean said suddenly as a man dressed in a tan raincoat and still wearing dark glasses came out of the cafe's rear entrance. He stood at the curb until a long yellow Jaguar, driven by a comely young woman with golden hair that hung to her shoulders stopped and he got in.

"It's Jo-Jo all right and he's got a new one," Jean commented.

"New car?"

"New blonde. He can't resist them."

Traffic was light at that hour and the car was sufficiently conspicuous so that Ken had no trouble following it to the avenue de la Grande Armée, around the Arc de Triomphe, and down the avenue Victor Hugo. Before it reached the avenue Henri

Martin it slowed down and turned off. Ken cruised slowly past what appeared to be a dead-end street.

"He's certainly picked an exclusive neighborhood. He must be in funds. You drive on and turn around," Jean said as he jumped out of the car. "I'll watch to see where they go in."

When Ken got back, Jean was standing waiting for him.

"They went in 21 *bis*. What shall we do? Either I can stay here while you go and telephone or—"

"It'll be better if you take the car and get to a telephone. I'll stay here to watch."

"Barring the unexpected, I don't think they'll come out any more tonight. I may have to go as far as the Place Victor Hugo to phone . . . everything around here looks shut up. I shouldn't be more than ten minutes."

But Ken had been waiting less than five minutes when the door of 21 *bis* opened and Jo-Jo unexpectedly came out. The American felt unpleasantly conspicuous as he turned to move slowly toward the avenue Victor Hugo. Jo-Jo walked past him and, crossing the street, gradually increased his pace while Ken did the same. When they came to the rue Mony, the gangster turned to the left where there was a maze of quiet little streets. Turning left again, he broke into a run, Ken following closely. Suddenly Jo-Jo stopped, wheeled around, and walked straight up to Ken, his gun glinting in the light from the street lamp. Ken reached for his own but he was too late. He did not recover consciousness for three days.

* * *

The first day Ken was ambulant, Stan Gavronski, his boss, dropped in to see him.

"They got Jo-Jo!" he announced, handing Ken a newspaper. "It's made the headlines and Jean is cock-a-hoop as all hell."

He dropped a pile of books and magazines on the bed. "And here. I've brought you these to read."

"Thanks, I've just about finished the last lot you brought. What happened? About Jo-Jo, I mean."

"History repeated itself. He couldn't keep away from the blonde."

"Had he spotted me? Was that why he came out?"

"He went out to get some cigarettes."

"Lord! So if I'd just stayed where I was he'd have come back and I'd have saved myself some mighty uncomfortable moments. Well, I couldn't know that."

"When do you expect to get out of here, Ken?" Gavronski asked, lighting a cigarette.

"Doctor says by the end of next week."

"That's swell. Say you take another couple of weeks to convalesce, you should be back at the office by the sixteenth."

Ken McCabe walked over to the window and stood looking out. Finally he turned.

"I've made up my mind, Stan. I'm not coming back," he said quietly.

"Not coming back! What the hell d'you mean?"

"Just what I say. I'm quitting the bureau."

"Chicken?" his boss asked softly, after a moment.

"Maybe partly," Ken replied, shrugging. "I sure got within hailing distance of the pearly gates. But it's not entirely that. I've been thinking of quitting for some time. This decided me."

"Why?"

The younger man walked about the room restlessly.

"Do you really believe in what we're doing, Stan?" he asked.

"This is a fine time to bring that up," the other replied bitterly. "Just before a top-level conference at which I'm supposed to tell those goons in Washington how the President's drug policy is turning up trumps all down the line."

"You won't have any trouble doing that. All those swell statistics show how improved Franco-U.S. cooperation has resulted in seizing so many more tons of dope this year than last, in effecting so many more arrests, etc. You can keep quiet about the fact that it's all not even the tip of the iceberg. But, just the same, it's all an expensive waste of time. If you can't stop people all over the world smuggling armored tanks, planes, and guns, which are bulky, to say the least, how are you going to stop them smuggling anything that takes as little room as fine powder?"

"You know the answer to that as well as I do. Get at the source of supply."

"Oh, balls. Dry up one source of supply and you get another. Dry up heroin and addicts take to something else."

"So what's the answer?"

"I don't have one—nothing that would win votes for politicians, that is. For me, the only answer is to write off the present addicts as a dead (and I mean dead) loss and legalize the sale of drugs to them. Let 'em have as much as they want."

"Yeah, and you'd get a new bunch of addicts."

"I doubt it. There's something about 'forbidden fruit' that's very tempting for the young. Perhaps we should make the sale of marijuana illegal . . . that's the least harmful and it would give the kids something to rebel against without causing as much harm as the strong stuff."

"What makes you think that if you legalize dope you won't get more addicts?"

"Stan, the pushers create the addicts . . . naturally . . . that's how they get damn rich damn quick. If heroin were available to addicts in any drugstore for the price of aspirin, that would be the end of the pushers and of the fantastic profits made by the dope barons."

"Oh, I've heard all that before. I don't believe it."

"You know as well as I do that the percentage of addicts, particularly mainliners, who are cured is almost zero. Also, it seems to me that what you do with your own life is your own business, not the government's. I'm not talking about kids, I'm talking about adults. If you want to commit suicide or become an alcoholic or a dope addict, it should be up to you. Warn and exhort, yes. But after that, leave the poor wretches alone to do what they want to do. If it's to kill themselves with dope, so be it. And legalizing dope would cut the crime rate by about fifty per cent, too, not to speak of the incomes of a lot of policemen and government officials."

"Well, I don't think your idea is going to get you anywhere.

It's a bit drastic. What are you going to do if you quit? You've made a pretty good career in government service so far."

"I haven't figured that one out, yet," McCabe admitted. "Of course, I *am* a lawyer. I suppose I could go back to North Dakota and hang out my shingle . . . perhaps go into politics. Come to think of it, that might be kind of fun. I might try to start a new party. The two we have both seem a bit moth-eaten."

"You may have an idea there, at that," Gavronski said. "When I get home this evening I'm going to have to spend most of the night working on the damned income tax. Find me a party that does away with all that paperwork and I'm with you."

"Why not a party that does away with taxes?"

"I guess you can't have a government without taxes."

"Why do we have to have so damn much government? There's lots of it we'd be better off without. We could start by eliminating the State Department . . . it doesn't seem much use. Then there's Agriculture . . . that's an expensive luxury; there's Justice . . . who'd know the difference if it weren't there? Come to think of it, it seems to me we could do away with most of the bureaucracy, including Narcotics. In fact, while we're at it, why not do away with an elected Congress, too. How about 'No taxation and no representation' as a slogan for our new party? Stan, I bet we'd sweep the country."

"You're a nut!" Gavronski laughed. "Who'd run the country if there were no Congress?"

"Oh, there'd be a Congress. Only, instead of electing representatives we'd appoint them the way we do a blue-ribbon jury, selecting outstanding, intelligent, sober citizens. They could serve three years and, of course, their jobs would be held open for them. No pay, just expenses and a little pocket money. More or less like draftees. Their chief job would be to take laws off the books, instead of passing more. Their other job would be to elect a president, probably one of themselves. Stan, you've had a swell idea and it's got infinite possibilities."

"It's your idea, not mine. Well, you work it out while you're waiting to get back to the bureau," Gavronski said as he got up. "It'll give you something to do."

"Stan, I told you. I'm not coming back. I meant it."

Gavronski moved toward the door.

"Don't make any decisions about quitting now," he said. "You've just had a bad time and you're tired out. Take a few weeks off and get some fresh air and sunshine and then think about it again. I'll bet you change your mind. And you've got to eat, remember."

"That doesn't bother me. Seems to me a man can always get a job."

"Don't be too sure. There's a lot of unemployment right now."

"There's always something. I read the other day about a school for butlers in London. I could take a course there and then make me some *real* money. Those guys can salt away about fifteen thousand dollars a year and live high on the hog at the same time. I'll never be able to do that in this racket. And you meet such interesting people. No, Stan, my mind is made up. I'm quitting."

"Well, I've got to go now. I still think you'll change your mind after you've thought it over. I'll be by to see you Sunday."

"My letter will have gone in by then."

"There's nothing more I can say, Ken. So long. Take care of yourself, boy."

Ken McCabe found he was weaker than he had realized and made only token resistance when the nurse told him it was time for him to go back to bed. As he relaxed against the pillows, the tray with his supper across his knees, he thought about his conversation with Stan Gavronski and wondered what he really *was* going to do with his life, eight years of which had been spent working for the government. Starting a new career at the age of thirty-two would not be easy. He had a little capital, what with the money he had been able to save and the forty thousand dollars his mother had left him. A small cattle spread? The idea did not appeal to him. A franchise of some sort? Starting his own law practice? He decided not to worry any more about it that day and glanced over the reading matter Stan Gavronski had brought him. There were several books that he might have enjoyed reading at some other time, but his head ached and he wanted something light, so he picked up a digest-size magazine and riffled through it. The articles did not seem to require concentration: the first one was addressed to women, telling them how to play their cards so as to pry a proposal of marriage from men who were plainly interested in nonmatrimony. Ken was a little surprised that they should want to go to so much trouble, his more recent reading having given him the impression that women now disdained marriage, considering it intolerable bondage.

The next article, lavishly illustrated with color photographs, seemed more promising. It was an account of the theft of the fabulous jewels of the Prince von Altberg-Emringen shortly after World War II during the Allied occupation of Germany. The theft, according to the article, was presumed to have been carried out by an American officer, quartered in the schloss, with or without the help of his WAC assistant, whom he had married in London and who had died under mysterious circumstances. In spite of the combined efforts of the U. S. Army and the police of different countries, not the slightest trace of Major George Zillitch or the jewels was ever found. The search for both was described in exhaustive detail and the prince, Ken learned, was willing to pay a handsome reward to anyone who could find out what happened to the thief and the jewels.

After reading the article, Ken turned to the illustrations. There were photographs of the more outstanding gems, of the safe they had been kept in, of the Schloss of Altberg-Emringen, of the prince and princess and their children, of Major George Zillitch and Edna Mae, both in uniform, and of the sandy beach in Cornwall where she had met her end.

Ken reread the article carefully four times. The next morning he wrote two letters, one resigning from the United States Narcotics Bureau and the other addressed to Prince Rupert von Altberg-Emringen.

CHAPTER VIII

White sand dunes extending on either side of the Auberge des Rochers embraced a bay and formed a small natural harbor the entrance to which was guarded by the weird rock formations that gave the inn its name. It was reconstructed from the ruins of a medieval monastery, its austerity relieved by window boxes of bright geraniums and the ivy covering its gray stone walls. Forged-iron gates led into a well-kept graveled courtyard made gay, at appropriate seasons, by massed rhododendron, azalea, lilac, and hydrangea bushes bordering a velvety lawn which the soft maritime climate of Brittany kept a brilliant emerald green all the year round. Broad steps leading to a terrace were guarded by two stone lions, and the name of the hotel was in discreet forged-iron characters over the front door.

The lobby, a vast, pillared room, had a frescoed vaulted ceiling. In it, modern comfort was successfully married to a sixteenth-century decor. Chintz-covered, down-filled armchairs and sofas were the ultimate in twentieth-century ease, but the chests, tables, and cupboards had the dark patina that only centuries of constant waxing and polishing can give.

The reception desk, formerly a pulpit, stood in a recess by the entrance. Its five sides were decorated with scenes of the Nativity in bas-relief while at the bottom of the central panel was carved the date A.D. MDCII. Beside it was a small switchboard.

It had taken the Auberge des Rochers two years to achieve its first Michelin star. Now, three years later, it had become a gourmet's Mecca and license plates from all over the world graced the Rolls-Royces, Mercedeses, Cadillacs and other gleaming monsters and aggressive sports cars that rubbed fenders in the courtyard.

The dining room itself had been the cloister of the old monastery. It was now roofed over, but on warm evenings the roof slid open and guests dined under the stars to the tinkle of the old fountain in the center of the pillared quadrangle. Here the walls were decorated with murals showing scenes of Breton life.

The blue and gold china used was specially made for the Auberge in Limoges, the crystal came from St. Louis and the tables were covered with silver lace cloths lined with blue silk, which matched the blue of the plates.

Oddly, for a restaurant in France, it was afternoon tea that had been at the origin of the Auberge's tremendous popularity. The little port of l'Aber-Wrac'h was much frequented by British yachtsmen, and it was they who first spread the word that here could be obtained the kind of afternoon tea now hard to find even in Britain.

Léonie had spent the six months before the Auberge was ready to receive its first guests in England, both for the language (useful in running a restaurant that hoped to attract an international clientele) and to find out whether there was anything worth learning about English cuisine; she discovered afternoon tea. So now people came to the Auberge in droves to feast on singin' hennies, fat rascals, scones, crumpets and crisp Scottish pancakes, all dripping butter and rich in calories. Léonie learned to make the clotted cream to use for Devonshire splits and to serve with strawberries in the summer, and she brought back recipes for saffron cake, crunchy shortbread, and dark, moist fruitcake. Tea bags were banned and tea was brewed in the homely brown earthenware pots connoisseurs claim give the best result.

George Simpson adored the teas and Léonie Lafauve always took special pains to make sure his crumpets and singin' hennies, his two favorites, were served piping hot and well buttered. She also had sent from Scotland the special strongly flavored heather honey to which he was partial.

It was, in fact, after a particularly copious tea that George, some months earlier, had had his first serious attack of acute indigestion. The local doctor who was called advised moderation, put him on a diet, and ordered that French panacea, Vichy water.

This April day Letitia Strong, a young American management trainee, was at the reception desk when Madame Ariane Simpson hurried into the lobby.

"I'm so sorry I had to keep you," she said as she came up to the desk.

"Is Mr. George better?" the girl asked. "I don't mind staying on if you'd rather not leave your husband." There was a lithe and controlled grace about the girl's slender body. The perfect arcs of her dark eyebrows over expressive gray eyes were her chief attraction—that and the soft cascade of her shoulder-length blond hair of a shade women dye for.

"Mademoiselle Léonie is keeping an eye on him. Anyway, he's much better and says he is feeling sleepy. I've talked to the doctor and he promised to stop in later this evening."

"Poor Mr. George! He's been sick so much lately."

"Yes," Ariane sighed. "I'm going to try to persuade him to take the cure at Vichy. He gets over these upsets when he sticks to a diet, but it's so difficult for him here. He does love good food!"

"I know!" Letitia replied feelingly. "Everything is so delicious it's hard to say no. I'm going to start to be firm with myself or I'll be as fat as a pig. I don't know how you keep so slim after years of eating Mademoiselle Léonie's cooking," she added as she looked admiringly at Ariane's slender form.

"It's like the people who work in chocolate factories—after a while they never touch the stuff. I think I must have reached that point; I never seem to be hungry any more."

"I wish I could say the same." Letitia gathered some papers together and stepped down from the desk.

"Is there anything new?" Ariane asked as she took her place.

"Lord and Lady Hardington are driving up from Paris and expect to get here in time for dinner. Their yacht arrives tomorrow. And that Mr. McCabe, who came yesterday, wanted to change his room again—that's the third time. I gave him twenty-two since he said he preferred to be at the back. Most people like the view of the sea. I made the change in the books."

Ariane nodded as she turned to answer the light on the switchboard and Letitia went up to her room.

Ten minutes later she let herself out of a back entrance of the inn that led directly into Mademoiselle Léonie's little private garden, which was also her hobby. It was in April that the garden was at its best, and Letitia paused to admire the lovely effect of the daffodils, narcissus, and iris that grew haphazardly in the grass under the trees, the neat beds of tulips, hyacinth, and pansies, and the lily of the valley and violets peeping out from under the shelter of lilac bushes. Taking the back road, she walked briskly toward the dunes, enjoying the feel of the misting rain on her face and breathing in the salt sea air.

Dotted over these dunes were indestructible reinforced-concrete casemates, pillboxes, gun emplacements, and dragon's teeth, all enduring testimony of the Hitlerean dream of Fortress Europa. Some day the sands of time would gently bury these and, to future generations, they might be as mysterious as Brittany's menhirs are today.

In front of one of the pillboxes, nature had contrived a natural seat, its concrete back softened by a sloping pillow of sand. This was Letitia's secret place, and here she hurried every day after lunch with a shopping bag containing the book she was reading and some writing materials. The walls of the pillbox behind her provided a shelter from wind and rain and before her lay the immensity of the ocean. She loved this spot, where she could either read, dreamily watch the waves, or work on her play.

Today, she was working on the play. In the night, she had had an inspiration as to how to handle an awkward place in Act II and her pen could barely keep up with the flood of insistent words.

"Well, you've certainly found yourself a cozy spot," an amused voice beside her said.

Letitia looked up with the exasperation any writer feels when interrupted while genius is burning brightly; she found herself being surveyed by a pair of small, alert blue eyes set in a thin tan face topped by tousled sandy hair. She recognized the hotel guest who had changed his room three times in two days.

"Oh, hello, Mr. McCabe."

"May I sit down?"

"By all means," Letitia replied without enthusiasm. "I hope you're finding your new quarters comfortable."

"Oh, very. I like the view on the garden. Cigarette?" And he held out a package.

"Thanks, but I don't smoke."

"I hope you don't mind if I do."

"Not at all."

"Are you Mr. Simpson's daughter?" Mr. McCabe asked as he lit his cigarette.

"Heavens, no! Why, poor Madame Ariane is only about thirty-five and I don't think she even looks that."

"How old is Mr. Simpson?"

"I don't know exactly. I should think in his fifties somewhere."

"Where does he come from?"

"He's an American, but I don't know from what part of the States. I think he lived in New York at one time."

"How did he happen to get into the hotel business here?"

"I suppose because he married a Frenchwoman."

"I don't believe I've seen Mr. Simpson since I've been here. Does he take any part in running the hotel?"

"He's been sick quite a bit lately. I believe he helped get the place started, but now he leaves it mostly to his wife and to Mademoiselle Léonie."

"Is she the woman who is always dressed in black slacks and black turtleneck sweater?"

"Yes, that's Mademoiselle Léonie. She's in charge of the restaurant. She's a marvelous cook."

"Is she Mrs. Simpson's sister?"

"Oh, no. I don't believe they're related at all. Just friends. But what gave you the idea that I was the Simpsons' daughter?"

"Well, you're an American, too, and you don't see many working in French hotels. Is this Madame Ariane Mr. Simpson's first wife?"

"So far as I know."

"How long have they been married?"

"I have no idea. But certainly not long enough to have a daughter my age."

"And what's your name?"

"Letitia Strong," she answered, beginning to feel annoyed at this interrogation.

"What's a pretty American girl like you doing in a dead hole like this? Couldn't you find a job somewhere more lively?"

Letitia was silent for a moment, then, after a nervous look around, she leaned toward Mr. McCabe.

"If you really want to know," she whispered, "I'm hiding."

"Hiding from whom?" McCabe asked.

Letitia tried desperately to think of a good follow-up. What do girls hide from in these permissive days? Certainly not an angry parent. And anyone hiding from the police would hardly take a perfect stranger into her confidence.

"My children's father," she finally brought out.

"Your husband?"

"He's not my husband. People don't get married much any more, do you think? I'm sure I never would."

"How many children do you have?"

"Four. Two boys and two girls."

"Four children! You don't look much more than a child yourself."

"My looks are deceptive. I'm twenty. And I had two sets of twins; Regan and Rosemary and Hillary and Hugh."

"Where are they?"

"I left them with Stavrides. It's awfully tiresome for him, of course, having them on his hands. The two eldest are only five and that's such an exhausting age. You have to run after them all the time and with four, each going in a different direction, it's simply killing. They can all climb out of and up onto anything."

"Why did you leave them?"

"But I've just told you. It was hell! Actually, I don't like children much. I've come to the conclusion that Herod is my favorite character in history."

"Why did you have children if you don't like them?"

"How was I to know I didn't like them until I'd had some? And at first they're not so bad—kind of cute, in fact. They sleep most of the time. I'd enjoyed playing with dolls when I was little and, of course, dolls don't grow up. It was only when Regan and Rosemary got bigger that I realized what a bore children are."

"But then you had another batch!"

"You make them sound like cookies. The second 'batch,' as you call them, were an accident. These things happen."

"So you're just going to abandon your children and leave them on Stavrides'—isn't that what you said his name was?—hands."

"They're his children, too," Letitia pointed out. "At least, I *think* they are."

"You *think* they are!" McCabe echoed, raising an eyebrow.

"Well, the postman was kind of cute and he had such a nice, tickly mustache," and Letitia gave a little shiver of remembered delight.

"I guess I'm a little out of touch with the youth of today," Ken remarked.

"It's the generation gap. Don't let it bother you," Letitia replied kindly. "We all have to get old. You look very well preserved."

"Thank you!"

"You're quite welcome!"

"Tell me, what does your Stavrides do?"

"He isn't *my* Stavrides. If he belongs to anybody, he belongs to Dulcina."

"And who is Dulcina?"

"Stavrides' wife. She must be simply hopping with rage."

"Oh! So Stavrides isn't opposed to matrimony per se?"

"He most certainly *is!* After you'd seen Dulcina, you wouldn't blame him."

"Why did he marry her, then?"

"Her father was the chief of police and he had six daughters to marry off with no dowries. In Greece, it's *very* hard to marry off daughters unless you can provide them with dowries, particularly ugly ones—daughters, I mean, not dowries. But Dulcina's father found a neat solution to his problem. You've got to hand it to the Greeks—they're certainly smart. This chief of police managed to get *all* his girls off his hands."

"What was his system?"

"Very simple, really. The best ideas usually are. He would arrange to have rich men's sons shadowed and, of course, nearly all of them did something that could be called criminal after a time. When he had the goods on them—hop—either they had to marry one of his daughters or they'd go to jail. And Greek jails aren't awfully comfortable."

"And what was Stavrides up to when he was caught?"

"Smuggling dope. He was just doing it till he had enough money to pay for a Ferrari he'd bought and smashed. He didn't dare go to his father because he'd told him he'd be disinherited if he smashed another car. Smuggling dope is by far the simplest way to lay your hands on a largeish sum of money. The trouble is that the Greeks are awfully stern about dope—life sentences or a firing squad or something. So poor Stavrides had to marry the most hideous of the six daughters. Sometimes he thinks he made the wrong choice—a firing squad would have been preferable. Now that Dulcina is landed with Ralph, Rosemary, Hillary and Hugh, she must be making his life a torment."

"*Regan* and Rosemary, not Ralph," he said, grinning. "You really should keep your children's names straight. Well, you've certainly got an imagination. You should be a writer."

Letitia's face lit up.

"Oh, I am. I mean, that is what I hope one day to be."

"What about the hotel business?"

"That's why I'm in it—partly, that is. You get to see such a lot of people, and a good many of them are real weirdies."

"What's the other part?"

"Oh, Pa owns a chain of motels in the States and I'm his eldest child so he wants me to learn the business. You've probably stayed at one of his places. It's almost impossible to avoid them. 'Strongholds,' Pa calls them, with repulsive little turrets all over them."

"Here we go again!"

"What do you mean?"

"Well, you're kind of given to romancing, aren't you?"

"I always tell lies when people start asking questions. Lying is a defense of privacy," Letitia answered placidly. "However, Pa really does own the Stronghold chain . . . at least, he owns a controlling interest."

"Your father is Josiah Strong?"

"Yes, and now I've got to go. I have to be back at the desk at six."

"Here, I'll carry that bag," Mr. McCabe said, falling into step beside her.

"That's all right. It's not heavy. How long are you planning to stay in l'Aber-Wrac'h?"

"It depends. Why?"

"Well, since you think it's such a 'dead' place, I can't see why you don't go somewhere gayer."

"I just meant it wasn't very lively for a young girl."

"It suits me," Letitia said shortly. There was a short silence as they walked along the sea front. The tide was coming in and the wind had freshened.

"Can you tell me—" Mr. McCabe began.

Letitia whirled on him, her gray eyes flashing.

"Did your grandmother keep geese?" she asked furiously.

"I believe so," the man replied urbanely. "Ducks, chickens, and guinea fowl, I'm sure about. I *think* she kept geese too. However, I gather you really don't care whether she did or not."

"Well, I don't want to be rude to a guest of the hotel but you've done nothing but ask questions. I'm simply not going to answer any more, Mr. McCabe."

"All right," the man said amiably. "My name is Kenneth, by the way; Ken to my friends. Would you like to drive in to Brest to the movies tonight?"

She was about to refuse the proffered olive branch but then hesitated. It had been some weeks since she had been to the cinema; the business of getting to Brest and back after dinner was something of a problem as she had no car.

"That would be very nice," she finally said. "We could go to see *The French Connection*. It just got a prize and I saw in the paper that it's playing in Brest."

Ken McCabe began to laugh. "You interested in narcotics?" he asked.

"Not particularly, but apparently the film's very exciting."

"Okay. We'll go and get excited with the rest of the folks."

As it happened, however, the projected jaunt did not come off. When they reached the Auberge, it was to find that George Simpson had suddenly taken a turn for the worse and Letitia could not be spared.

CHAPTER IX

The first years the Simpsons and Léonie Lafauve worked together had gone relatively smoothly. George had provided, besides all the considerable capital needed, an expertise about running a hotel which contributed largely to its success. Various of his devices which both increased the comfort of the guests and resulted in savings of labor were, in fact, later to be adopted by big new hotels that sprang up in Paris a few years later. But as suddenly as he had undertaken the venture, George Simpson lost all interest in it, and the hidden mutual antipathy between her husband and her old friend which Ariane had vaguely sensed gradually became more and more manifest.

The change had started at the time the Auberge achieved its first star and now, two years later, with a second star well within reach, it had become very obvious even though it took the form of excessive politeness between the two antagonists and deferral to each other, particularly on the part of Léonie, who felt, with some justification, that the inn's success was due chiefly to her own labors in the kitchen, creating and perfecting culinary masterpieces.

Without knowing just why, Ariane felt vaguely to blame, though she could think of no particular sins of either commission or omission toward either. During the past six months, when George had gone from one bout of illness to another and required a good deal of her attention and care, Léonie had taken on a martyred air which Ariane found both irritating and exhausting. And whenever she left George to help Léonie with the business of running the hotel, her husband waxed sarcastic. In fact, Ariane felt uncomfortably like a bone between two dogs.

As she sat beside her husband's bed after his latest attack, she thought about her own relations with him. These had also altered; his physical demands on her had gradually lessened and, as she leaned back in the chair and closed her eyes, she realized that it had been over six months since he had made love to her. This was not a matter of particular regret to her since her response had always been prompted by her gratitude to him and a sense of duty rather than desire. His increasing girth, too, made their relations less satisfactory even to him. However, the fact that he no longer needed her physically made her devote even more time and attention to his care and comfort. But she was still a young woman and this fact undoubtedly accounted for the incident of the previous week. Resolutely she tried to shut out the recollection of the lean hard body against hers, of the gaze of the dark, smoldering eyes, of the strong lips pressing hard on hers and, finally, of her own eager response.

"Oh, God!" she groaned to herself. "Things can't go on like this. Where is it all going to end?" And she got up and walked restlessly to the window.

Because of George's increased weight and various illnesses, Ariane had decided it would be more practical to move their private apartment down to the ground floor to eliminate the chore of carrying things up and down stairs all day long. She had selected two rooms that gave directly onto the garden in the back of the Auberge, and the french windows opened onto a little terrace where George liked to sit. As she leaned her aching head on the cool glass, she thought she saw a dark figure duck into the trees that edged Léonie's garden. She opened the window wider and, stepping outside, peered into the night. She could see no one. It could, she supposed, have been Léonie, and she called her name in a low voice. There was no answer. Ariane glanced at her watch to find it was three thirty in the morning. If it was Léonie, it was an odd hour for her to be up and dressed. But it was an equally odd hour for any of the hotel guests to be up and about.

A sound from the bed made her turn around and she hurried over to her husband's side to find him awake.

"How do you feel?" she asked anxiously, bending down to straighten the covers.

"I'm thirsty," he muttered.

"What would you like? An orangeade?"

He nodded and Ariane went out to the kitchen. She met Léonie in the hall.

"Oh, you're up. So it was you I saw in the garden," she said.

"I haven't been in the garden," Léonie replied. "I've just come downstairs. How is George?"

"He seems to be a bit better. He's awake and thirsty. I'm going to get him a glass of orangeade."

"I'll get it, Ariane. You're looking exhausted. When I bring it, let me stay with him till morning while you go up to my room and get some rest."

Ariane shook her head.

"I'm not so tired; I've slept off and on. Dr. LeBlanc is coming early, and if he finds George well enough, he's going to send an ambulance to take him to the hospital for some new tests before noon. I'll catch up on my sleep while George is away."

"You go back, then, while I get the orangeade."

But Ariane stood, a slight frown on her face.

"If it wasn't you in the garden, I wonder who it was, at this hour," she said.

"Was it a man or a woman?"

"I couldn't really tell. Whoever it was was all in black, which was why I thought it was you."

"It wasn't me. As I said, I haven't been out. You're overtired. Perhaps you imagined it."

"Well, perhaps," Ariane replied with a shrug and returned to her husband.

A few minutes later there was a light tap at the door and Léonie handed Ariane a tray with a cup of tea and a glass of orangeade.

"I've made the orangeade fairly sweet; sugar is strengthening," Léonie said. "The tea is for you. Drink it while it's hot."

"Oh, that's just what I need," Ariane answered, smiling her

thanks. "There's no reason for us both to be up. You go back to bed, Léonie."

"I'm not tired. If you want anything, I'll be in the office." The martyred tone crept back into her voice. "I am, of course, glad to do all the work while you take care of your husband. But there are only twenty-four hours in the day—I have to use what time I find available."

"I hope the worst is over now," Ariane sighed. "Thank you, Léonie."

Ariane closed the door and set the tray down. The tea was still too hot to drink so she took the orangeade over to George and, helping him to sit up, she put the glass to his lips.

"Don't do that," he said crossly, pushing her hand away. "I'd rather hold it myself."

Ariane stuffed another pillow behind his back as she handed him the glass. Then, picking up her cup, she began to sip her tea.

"How is the orangeade?" she asked.

"It's cold and it's wet," he answered. Ariane finished her tea and George handed her his nearly empty glass; she set both back on the tray.

"I think I'll go to sleep again, now," George said. "Can you take some of this stuff away so that I can lie down? You go to bed, too," he went on as Ariane removed the extra pillows from behind his head. "I feel better. Turn out the light and get some rest yourself."

"Don't worry about me," she said, kissing his forehead. "All I want you to worry about is getting well."

"You're a good girl, Ariane, a real good girl," George said, giving her hand a squeeze. Then he turned on his side and closed his eyes.

Ariane set the tray on the floor outside the door, turned out the light, stretched out on the twin bed, and soon fell into a deep sleep.

*   *   *

Letitia was getting tired. Except for a half-hour break for some dinner, she had worked through the evening and, looking at the clock, she was relieved to see it was nearly time for the night porter to come on duty.

Ken McCabe was having a long-drawn-out coffee and after-dinner brandy in the lounge and she was conscious of the fact that, in spite of the magazine he held open in front of him, his eyes were frequently on her. Finally he sauntered over to the reception desk.

"It's nearly ten," he said. "Are you planning to work all night?"

"Not if I can help it. I'll be through in a few minutes."

"Sit down and have a drink with me."

"The hired help aren't supposed to mingle with the guests."

"I've got my car outside. We could go somewhere else."

"I really can't," Letitia replied. "I'm kind of pooped. And I expect it'll be just as bad tomorrow. I'd better get to bed."

"Who takes over when you leave? Is there someone on duty here all night?"

"The night porter stays at the desk till all the guests have either left or gone to bed. There's a little room back of this one where he has a cot. He hears if someone comes to the front door or if the phone rings. Here he is now." And Letitia closed the book she was reading, stood up, and stretched her arms down her sides. "Golly, I'm stiff."

"Sure I can't talk you into any form of dissipation?"

"Not tonight you can't. I'll take a rain check."

"In that case I'll say good night. Guess I'll go for a short walk before turning in."

Ken walked along the road that skirted the sea wall; the tide was in and he could hear the slap of the waves on the rocks below. After about ten minutes, he turned to the left and took a path that led to the back of the grounds of the Auberge. The gate at the back entrance was locked. Picking the lock was the work of a minute and, taking the precaution of oiling the hinges liberally to prevent any telltale sound, Ken let himself into the garden. With the aid of binoculars, he was able to look into the

various rooms. Finally he found what he wanted and he kept
his binoculars trained on the Simpsons' room, where Ariane was
sitting beside her husband's bed. Silently he made his way out
of the grounds and, returning to the hotel by the front door, he
went up to his room, saying good night to the porter as he passed
the reception desk.

Ken McCabe took a packet of photographs from the false bottom of his suitcase and went through them quickly. Finally he
found the two pictures he was looking for. One was of a couple
standing arm in arm. The man, somewhat florid of face, wore a
white carnation in his buttonhole. The woman, who looked to
be about thirty, had on a lace dress and jacket and a floppy lace
hat and carried a bouquet of flowers cradled in her left arm.
What interested Ken about the picture was the diamond ring
she had on, and he peered at it carefully with a powerful magnifying glass. Then he compared it to the other two photographs
of diamond rings; one lay by itself on a black velvet cushion and
every facet was clearly visible in the enlargement. The second
seemed to be exactly like the first except that this time it was on
a woman's hand. Ken had taken the photograph himself with a
concealed camera the day before when he passed the reception
desk while Ariane was sitting at it. To a layman's eye, the three
pictures seemed to be of the same ring.

The rest of the photographs seemed to be of the same man
and, picking them up one at a time, he subjected each to
a thorough scrutiny. Then he sighed. He had examined these so
frequently that he could conjure up the face with his eyes shut.
What he desperately wanted was to get a look at the man who
called himself George Simpson. But George Simpson had been
shut up in his room ever since Ken's arrival.

It was about two o'clock when he put the photographs away,
took off his outer garments and shoes, and donned black trousers,
sweater, and tennis shoes, and slipped black silk gloves on his
hands. Taking his binoculars, his pencil flashlight, and his infrared movie camera with telescopic lens, he stepped out into the
corridor. Except for a guest snoring in one of the other rooms,
there was no sound. He moved down the service stairs, which

led to a side door into the grounds. Quietly he unlocked this and stepped into the garden. The light in the Simpsons' room was the only one on. Taking cover behind a rhododendron bush, he prepared for a lengthy vigil. For a long time nothing happened; both Ariane and her husband seemed asleep. He moved toward the Auberge to get a better view into the room when suddenly Ariane got to her feet and came toward the window. Ken McCabe ducked behind a bush when he saw her step out on to the terrace and peer into the dark.

"Is that you, Léonie?" she called in a low voice. Finally she went back into her room.

Ken looked about for a suitable observation post. The tree branches were too high up for him to reach them without a ladder and the trunks were too thick for him to swarm up one. Behind the bushes, however, he found a tool shed and from its roof had an excellent view into the bedroom. He sat there patiently, his camera trained on Ariane's movements. He watched her go out of the room, then come back a few minutes later. He caught a glimpse of a pair of hands as a tray was passed to Ariane, and he saw her give her husband the glass of orangeade. When a few minutes later she stooped down to set the tray outside the bedroom door, Ken suddenly had an idea. He jumped to the ground and hurried back into the Auberge, remembering to lock the door behind him. His tennis shoes made no sound as he walked quickly down the corridor that led to the Simpsons' apartment, lighting the way with his tiny flashlight. He found the tray outside the door and picked up the glass, holding it carefully by the rim.

When he got back to his room, he set the glass on the table. Locking his door and making sure the curtains at the windows were well closed, he took a box out of a valise. Spraying a fine gray powder over the glass he watched, his eyes bright with excitement, as fingerprints manifested themselves. There were several. Taking glossies of enlarged prints out of an envelope, with his magnifying glass he compared them with those on the glass, subjecting each to the same intense examination. Finally

he sat back and, like Archimedes in his bath, exclaimed,
"Eureka!"

*   *   *

Ariane, the next morning, was wakened by a knocking at the
door. Pushing the eiderdown back, she slipped her feet into
mules. The knock was repeated.

"I'm coming," she called as she looked at her watch and was
surprised to find how long she had slept: it was after eight
o'clock.

A man carrying a doctor's satchel was standing at the door
when she opened it. Had it not been for the satchel, one would
have taken him for a sailor. He was dressed in a heavy blue high-
necked sweater, blue trousers, and espadrilles. A thatch of graying black hair, as though tousled by the wind, surmounted a
weather-beaten, craggy face. A scar on his forehead lifted one
eyebrow, giving him a perpetually sardonic look which was belied
by laughter lines at the corners of his bright black eyes. Dr. Le-
Blanc had, in fact, been in the French Navy before retiring to his
native Brittany, where he spent what time he could wrest from
his practice on his passion for sailing.

"I'm so sorry, I seem to have overslept," Ariane said, trying
to smooth down her hair.

"How is your husband?"

"I think he's better. He only woke up once in the night when
he said he was thirsty. I gave him something to drink and he
went right back to sleep. And he's still asleep."

"I'll have a quick look at him, and if he's well enough, we'll
have him in the hospital again for some more tests."

"George," Ariane called, turning toward the bed. "It's time to
wake up. Dr. LeBlanc is here."

But there was no answer from the bed for the very good reason
that George was dead.

CHAPTER X

Ken McCabe went to bed but was too excited to sleep. As dawn was breaking, he took a bath, dressed, tiptoed downstairs, and let himself out of the hotel without rousing the night porter. Getting into his car, he placed a small box in which he had packed the purloined glass on the seat beside him and settled down to the long drive to Paris. From the first open post office he came to, he telephoned Jean Labruyère and arranged to meet him for lunch at the apartment. He then telegraphed the Prince von Altberg-Emringen.

As Ken drove on, he thought over the events of the eight months that had elapsed since his resignation from the United States Bureau of Narcotics and his first meeting with the Prince von Altberg-Emringen. This meeting had taken place in Düsseldorf, where the prince was the head of Altberg Gebauverein GmbH, a highly successful construction company. On his return from Russia, the young man had been appalled by the sight of the once-proud cities of his native land lying in blackened ruins in which people still lived, taking shelter wherever two walls could be roofed over, a potted geranium bravely glowing in front of a blasted window. It seemed to him that building was the crying, immediate need and, with the proceeds of the sale of two of the famous Altberg-Emringen Impressionist paintings, started a building firm which, over the years, had prospered mightily. Within five years, he succeeded in buying back his paintings for three times what he had sold them for.

Ken and the prince had liked each other from the beginning, and the German had appreciated the fact that Ken requested no expense money even though the search for Major Zillitch might well prove a costly one.

"That's my gamble," the American had replied when the prince brought up the subject. "But if I do find Zillitch and track down the jewels—"

"Fifty-fifty," the prince promised.

"That's too much," Ken demurred. "Anyway, we can discuss the matter when and if I succeed. No good ever comes of counting chickens before they're hatched."

"What makes you think you have a chance of finding Zillitch now, when the trail is cold, when the police of many countries and the American Army failed to do so just weeks after the theft?"

Ken shrugged.

"In the first place, I'm quite good at putting myself in another man's skin; it was the reason for my relatively good record as a narcotics agent. In the second place, I doubt very much that the Army wanted to find Zillitch. Stan Gavronski, my boss in Paris, used to be with the Army in Heidelberg after the war. He remembers the case well. Stan says that, while the looting by U.S. personnel was not on the wholesale, systematic scale practiced by the Russians, there were a good many light-fingered gentry in our service, too, and it was not always only the men. The wives got in the act also. So it seems possible that the Army went out of its way *not* to find Major Zillitch; he probably would have been able to point a finger at quite a few people and cause embarrassment. I'm counting quite heavily on this."

The German invited Ken to spend a weekend at the schloss and here he was shown the safe, now empty, behind the secret panel. The two men also spent hours studying the colored photographs of the gems which the prince's father had had the foresight to have taken.

"They've probably been recut by this time, though," Ken said, gazing at a marquise diamond on a black velvet cushion. "It's too bad that the Identigem system wasn't invented in your father's time."

"What is the Identigem system?"

"Gemmologists have discovered that diamonds are like fingerprints—no two are alike. A company has now been set up to start a databank of diamond 'fingerprints.' If your father could have had these diamonds logged, there would be no difficulty in identifying them should we be lucky enough to track them down, even if they had been recut."

"That's very interesting. I must tell my wife—she has a few nice diamonds. Where do you think Major Zillitch concealed the jewels that he took?"

"Well, Switzerland isn't far. Putting myself in his shoes, that's where I would have gone. I would have rented a safe-deposit box in some bank there."

"Do you think they might still be there?"

"I imagine he converted them into money . . . which he may well have used to start a business."

"So, even if you find him, it will be difficult to prove the theft. And what about the statute of limitations?"

"If I find Zillitch and he does have money he can't account for, he can be forced to surrender it even if he escapes a jail sentence due to the statute of limitations. Anyway, you have to bear in mind that there is no statute of limitations for murder, and the police in England had a warrant out for Zillitch for the murder of his wife. I believe we can make things quite hot for the worthy major. But, as the cookbook says, 'first catch your hare.' I think I'd better get started doing just that." And Ken stood up to go.

"Let me know how you get on," the prince said, walking with him to the front door. "I'll be very much interested in hearing even if you are not successful. How do you actually rate your own chances?"

Ken shrugged.

"I'd say I have about a twenty-five-per-cent chance. One out of four is a pretty good gamble."

* * *

Ken McCabe began his search in Washington and ran into his first serious obstacle when he attempted to obtain from the Pentagon the file on Major Zillitch, which, inexplicably, was classified top secret even though it concerned events that had occurred over a quarter of a century earlier and which in any event could hardly be considered as vital to U.S. security. Princess von Altberg-Emringen, when informed of the problem, appealed to her uncle, Senator O'Neill, still a powerful figure on Capitol Hill though an octogenarian, and it was only through his insistence that Ken had been permitted, with the greatest reluctance, to examine the file, out of which he succeeded in abstracting the card on which were recorded the prints of the major's ten fingers. He also surreptitiously removed several photos.

From the morgue of one of the capital newspapers, he got the complete news coverage of the story, and this he found far more helpful than the Defense Department files.

Then he settled down to the search in earnest. It led him from New England to New York, back to Washington, to Germany, to Chicago, back to Washington and New York again and, finally, to Costa Rica.

The first break had come when he was checking on the major's parents. The building in which they had had their grocery store had been torn down some fifteen years earlier and an up-to-date car wash and filling station stood in its place. Nobody could tell Ken what had happened to the two Zillitches, but an examination of the courthouse records showed they had died within months of each other while their son was in the Army. Further search of the records showed that on March 12, 1921, Jacob Zillitch had married one Adela, daughter of William and Catherine Simpson, born in Chicago in 1894. Ken checked back on George's date of birth, which, according to the Army records, was June 3, 1915. Couples frequently marry after the birth of a child, but six years seemed an unusually long time to wait. Moreover, there was no record of the birth, either legitimate or illegitimate, of a George Zillitch, or even, should he have been registered under his mother's name, of a George Simpson in 1915.

Ken flew to Chicago to check on Adela Simpson and found the registration of her birth in 1894. Turning to 1915, Ken finally found what he was looking for. Thomas, son of William and Catherine Simpson, and his wife, Jessie, recorded the birth of their son, George, on June 3 of that year. The following year both Thomas and Jessie were killed in an accident. Presumably, then, his aunt and her husband undertook to raise him without the formality of adoption. Ken thought he now at least knew the name of the man he was looking for.

In Washington, he learned that the State Department had issued a passport to a George Simpson in 1948, and here Ken had another stroke of luck: he discovered that a classmate of his was working in the Passport Division. From him he found out that an application for renewal had come, in 1952, from the United States consulate in Costa Rica. So Ken flew to Costa Rica.

Among the foreign colony there were a good many people who remembered George Simpson, particularly his prowess as a trencherman.

"He wasn't any kind of a drinker," the secretary of the American Club said, "but, God, he was a heavy eater. He left here—let's see, it must have been around 1952, but I have no idea where he went. He was always kind of a closemouthed sort of guy and we used to wonder where he was from and why he came to Costa Rica. You might talk to Wanda Liebermann; she took over his bookstore."

Wanda Liebermann turned out to be a parchment-faced, ageless American woman whose green eyes peered nearsightedly out of thick-lensed pince-nez, secured by a chain to a straight cotton garment that reached her sandaled feet.

"I didn't have much money when I took the store over," she said, rattling the bracelets that covered both thin arms as she talked, "so I offered to pay George for the stock and good will out of receipts, so much a month. But he said not to bother. I finally managed to raise five hundred dollars and gave him that. The stock, though, was worth several times that amount."

"He didn't talk about his plans?"

"Not a word. All I can tell you is that he said he intended to live in the country that had the best food in the world. Since it's kind of hard for a foreigner to settle down in China these days, I suppose he meant France."

On his way to France, Ken stopped in England. From the

newspaper clippings he had studied, he knew that George Zillitch's marriage to Edna Mae had taken place at the Chelsea Registry Office. It occurred to him that brides usually like to be photographed, at the time of their marriage, in their wedding finery. He went to Chelsea with the intention of visiting all the photographic studios in the district. But he got the right place on his second try and was able to obtain a picture of the bridal pair.

Ken McCabe, convinced that his quarry was somewhere in France, blessed French bureaucracy. That vast organization, a gigantic sponge to absorb France's ever-increasing number of otherwise unemployable university graduates, had files on all foreign residents. The tax records were particularly fruitful. Under French law, married couples' tax returns are filed jointly, and a woman, unless she is divorced or widowed, may not sign her own; even though she generates all the income, the return must be signed by the husband. Ken, with the assistance of Jean Labruyère, found that George Simpson had, in the first years he lived in France, been taxed as a single man according to a formula the tax authorities use to assess foreigners living in France whose source of income is outside the country. This formula is based on the amount of rent paid and the standard of living displayed. Later, however, the tax return had been a joint one, signed by George Simpson, though the income, during the last two years a substantial one, had been derived from a hotel owned by his wife, Ariane, née Quatsous. Thus, at last, Ken had run the missing major to earth at the Auberge des Rochers, in l'Aber-Wrac'h.

* * *

As Ken drew up in front of the apartment house, he saw Jean coming across the street and waved.

"You sounded excited on the telephone this morning," Jean said as they went upstairs.

"I was. In fact, I still am!"

"You really think this George Simpson is the man you are looking for?"

"I'm sure of it—more than that, I know it."

"Come in to the kitchen and you can tell me about it while I fix us a drink and finish getting lunch. Did I tell you I have replaced the old kitchen stove with one of these modern electric ones which are automatic? I put my lunch in the oven before I leave in the morning and, hey, presto, it is ready for me at noon. It's like a miracle! You can't say we French aren't modern now."

They walked into the kitchen and Jean proudly displayed his gleaming acquisition; Ken did not have the heart to tell him his mother had had the same type of stove in America twenty years earlier. Jean poured out a whiskey and soda for each of them.

"To your health, and particularly to your wealth," he said as he raised his glass. "Now tell me."

As Ken gave an account of what had happened, Jean took the boeuf bourguignonne out of the oven, prepared a salad, and set out cheese and fruit.

"So you haven't actually seen this Mr. Simpson yet?" he asked as they sat down at the table.

"No. And I'm afraid the photographs I got of him with my infrared camera won't be very conclusive. He was lying in bed and his face was turned away from the window most of the time. But there's no doubt about the fingerprints and that's where I need your help. I have to have those fingerprints identified officially. Do you think you can arrange that?"

"Well, I don't know," Jean replied after a moment's thought. He poured out some wine. "The French police are not going to be very interested in a theft that took place over twenty-five years ago of German property in Germany by an American."

"I realize that. But do you have to explain why you need an identification of the fingerprints? Couldn't you say your service was interested in the background of this man? That you thought he might be connected with a dope ring?"

"I suppose that is possible. I have a cousin who works at the Quai des Orfèvres. I'll go to see him tomorrow."

"You couldn't do it today?"

"Perhaps I could if I leave right away. I have an appointment later. Will you wait for me here?"

"I think I'll drive right back, Jean," Ken said. "I don't want to miss an opportunity of seeing this George Simpson even if I have to break into his room. Here's the box with the glass. Be careful with it—remember it's worth its weight in diamonds! As soon as you have any news, telephone me at the Auberge des Rochers, l'Aber-Wrac'h. I'll be waiting to hear from you."

"I'll give you a ring as soon as I can."

It was after ten when Ken finally got back to l'Aber-Wrac'h. Letitia was still at the desk.

"Oh, there you are!" she exclaimed.

"Don't tell me that you've missed me!"

"It isn't that I've missed you—I haven't had time. But you asked so many questions about Mr. Simpson I thought you'd be interested to know that he has died. God, things are in a mess!"

"What!" Ken exclaimed.

"Yes. Isn't it awful?" And she turned to still the buzzing telephone.

CHAPTER XI

For Ariane, the day of her husband's death had a quality of unreality. She felt like a person who had accidentally strolled into the middle of someone else's nightmare. Nothing that went on had any connection with her. She heard what was said but the words had no meaning or relevance, and it did not even seem strange to her that Léonie should choose this moment to badger her about a lost drinking glass.

"It was one of the two blue goblets you bought me for Christmas six years ago. Can't you remember what you did with it?" Léonie asked, for the third time.

"Did with what?"

"The glass with the orange juice!" And Léonie had to control herself to keep from shouting the words.

Ariane looked uncomprehending.

"No thank you, Léonie, I don't want any orange juice. I don't want anything. Please go away," she answered.

Finally left alone, Ariane stood a long time at the window, staring into the garden. There was a light tap at the door, followed by the sound of its opening, but Ariane did not move.

"I have to go now," the doctor said, setting down his satchel and walking over toward her. "I've talked to the undertakers and the funeral will be on the day after tomorrow. Is there anything more I can do for you? Would you like a sedative?"

Ariane shook her head, then turned around.

"Tell me one thing. Would it have made any difference if I had stayed awake?"

"None."

"How did he die?"

"The way we all die, Ariane. His heart stopped beating."

"Of course I know George died because his heart stopped beating," Ariane said impatiently. "What I want to know is why it stopped beating just at that point. You said yourself earlier in the evening that he was recovering. And he seemed even better later on. Oh, if I'd only not gone to sleep!"

Dr. LeBlanc put his hands out to touch her, then let them drop to his sides.

"Ariane, you must believe me when I tell you that it was only because your husband had an iron constitution that he lived as long as he did. A less basically healthy person would have died years earlier. As much as any man ever did, your husband dug his grave with his teeth. He'd overstrained his heart for decades and it finally stopped while he was asleep. It's a peaceful way of going; I hope I shall be as lucky. You were a good wife and did more than your duty."

"Yes," Ariane said simply. "I had to, you see. Because I could not give George my love, I had to give him everything else possible. I can't bear to think that in the end I may have failed him."

"You didn't fail him," the doctor said roughly. "There's no reason for you to wear that hair shirt the rest of your life."

"'The rest of my life,'" Ariane repeated. "It sounds like a long sentence . . . to emptiness. A woman has to be needed and George needed me. I have learned that you should never marry someone you don't love because it makes you feel guilty and there's two 'you's' and you begin to hate each other. George used to come between us and now there's nobody. The two 'me's' will have to spend the rest of our lives together." And she turned back to the window.

"The two 'you's' will have to patch up your differences and become friends." There was tenderness in his eyes as he looked at her, but he spoke lightly. "To talk about more practical matters, do you want me to take you to the *mairie* to register your husband's death?"

"I'd rather go alone. Also, I suppose I should buy some mourning. George hated to see me in black, so I don't have one single thing I can wear to the funeral."

"Well, I'll send the death certificate around as soon as I can. You are sure you wouldn't like something to make you sleep?"

"No, thank you."

"Shall I call Mademoiselle Lafauve?"

"No, I want to be alone. I think I want to pray . . . pray for George and pray for me."

The doctor raised Ariane's hand to his lips with a quick gesture and left the room.

*   *   *

Mademoiselle Léonie invariably made an inspection tour of the kitchen and dining room before every meal, and the death of Ariane's husband did not cause her to alter her routine. If anything, she was more meticulous than usual, even going so far as to open and close seldom used drawers and cupboards.

As she entered the dining room the waitresses, who had been talking in subdued tones as they worked, fell silent when they saw her, and the only sound was the clink of plates and glasses as they were placed on the tables covered with blue-lined silver lace cloths.

The manager walked from table to table checking on the gleam of the china, of the crystal goblets and of the silver. One glass revealed a smear as she held it to the light. Without a word she handed it to the waitress beside her, who scurried away to replace it. Such was the dampening effect of Mademoiselle Léonie's presence that even after she had left the room the waitresses continued silent as they went about their tasks.

From the dining room, the manager went into the kitchen. Here a cook was feeding raw lobster, filleted pike, and thick cream into a large blender, which he emptied from time to time into a bowl. Mademoiselle Léonie watched as he seasoned this mixture, which was to be used to stuff the turbot, waiting, in their round pans, to be placed in the vast coal-burning ovens.

"Add a little sherry," Mademoiselle Léonie suggested, tasting the mixture. She passed on to the dessert table at which a young girl was beginning to cover a row of chocolate pies, the crusts of which were a hardened chocolate-and-ground-almond mixture and the fillings a chocolate mousse covered with whipped cream. Mademoiselle Léonie tasted the cream and frowned.

"I told you to use bitter almond flavoring, not vanilla, Suzanne," she said harshly.

"Oh, dear!" the girl said contritely. "I'm so sorry. I forgot."

"Well, throw that away and prepare some fresh."

Suzanne looked sulky.

"Couldn't we use the vanilla just this one time? It's always been vanilla before and everyone loved it."

"Don't make me repeat myself. I told you to throw it away and make fresh. And the cost of the extra cream will come out of your pocket. That should teach you not to forget my instructions."

The years had not been unkind to Léonie Lafauve. Besides having the hair on her upper lip removed, she had shed about thirty superfluous pounds so that the black slacks, shoes, and turtleneck sweater she so invariably wore became her well. Her hair, now nearly white, she still wore in a crew cut and, combined with her restless black eyes under bushy graying brows and her high-bridged, imperious nose, the face was a striking one.

Back in her own office she sat down at her desk and drew toward her the large vellum-bound book in which a copy of the menu for every meal served at the Auberge des Rochers was preserved. Carefully she fitted the day's two menus into the slots on the thick pages and replaced the volume beside similarly bound ones, each marked with a different year, on the bookshelf behind her. She looked at them for a moment, and passed a hand caressingly over them. Then she got up and bolted her door. Taking her keys from her pocket, she selected one and unlocked a desk drawer, from the back of which she drew out a small box. With another key which she wore on a chain around her neck, she opened this and removed two little medicine bottles it contained, went into the bathroom, and emptied their contents into the toilet, which she flushed repeatedly. The two empty bottles she smashed with a hammer on the tile floor, using a woolen sweater to deaden the sound. Carefully collecting the smithereens, she put them in an empty matchbox, which she pocketed for later disposal.

Everything was now taken care of—except to find the glass, to find the glass, to find the glass, and the words repeated themselves endlessly as she paced the floor in an agony of frustration. What could have happened to it? she asked herself for the thousandth time. Her mind went over the events of the night before. After preparing the tray and giving it to Ariane, she had gone back to her room and waited at the window until she saw the light in the Simpsons' bedroom go out. She had then gone at once to pick up the tray. It was dark in the corridor and she had not realized the glass was missing until she reached the kitchen and had turned on the light. She had been worried but reflected that perhaps George had not drunk all the orangeade and consequently that Ariane had left the glass on the night table. She carefully washed out and dried the cup that had contained Ariane's tea, to which she had added a soporific. For a few moments she had toyed with the idea of slipping into the bedroom to remove the glass but remembered that Ariane invariably locked the door. Finally she reflected that, assuming that the events of the next few hours would go as she had planned them, it would be quite simple for her to pick up the glass as soon as George's death was discovered. Provided the glass was still on the night table.

Léonie had not gone to bed that night and, in the morning, had kept an eye on the Simpsons' bedroom, waiting for the outburst she felt sure would occur. Finally, she saw Dr. LeBlanc knock at the door and go in the room. Léonie waited for the summons she knew must come and when it did, she hurried into the room. Ariane had sunk down on the floor beside her husband's bed and, even as Léonie spoke to her, her eyes had darted quickly to the night table. There was no glass there. As soon as she could, she went into the bathroom. Here, too, she had drawn a blank, even though she went back repeatedly, checking every cupboard and even looking through the laundry basket.

What could have happened to it? Glasses do not just dematerialize. If it had been broken, she would have found the pieces.

While the recovery of the goblet was of paramount importance to Léonie, she realized that it would be foolish to ask any more questions about it. She would continue her search in silence.

*   *   *

It was after ten and the last guest had left the dining room when Léonie walked along the corridor to Ariane's room and went in. Ariane, at the desk, was going through her late husband's papers and looked up as her friend came in.

"Well, that's the end of another day," Léonie said, sitting down in the chair beside the desk. "Are you looking for something?"

"Not really," Ariane answered. "I know that George had no immediate family, but it occurred to me that he might have distant cousins or old friends who should know he had died. I was looking through his things to see if I could find old letters or other papers."

"In all these years, we've never seen a relative or even anyone who had ever known him, have we?"

"N-n-no. But this is a pretty out-of-the-way place."

"That's nonsense. People from all over come here. We're getting as well known as the Pyramides at Vienne or Baumanière at Les Baux," Léonie said. "Did George ever tell you exactly how he made his money?"

"He was in various businesses, including, of course, the hotel business."

"What about a will?" Léonie asked.

"I haven't found one. But perhaps he had nothing to leave. After all, he spent over five million francs on the Auberge and, in addition, kept it going the first years before it began to show a profit."

"One year," Léonie amended. "It began to show a profit the second year."

"That still might have used up all his capital. And, since he put the Auberge in my name, there would be no need for a will."

"Nonsense! No man would leave himself penniless and dependent on his wife. There must be money somewhere. Where did he bank?"

"You know he never had a bank account here, that he always paid for everything in cash."

"Then there is certainly a bank account in some other country —probably in the United States."

"Perhaps I'll find something in his papers. But I really don't care much."

"That is foolish. If George has left money, you should be the one to have it.

"I've been thinking, Ariane, that it would be sensible for me to move my things down here and share this apartment with you, now that George has gone. It would give us an extra room and bath for guests—that would bring in about another ten to fifteen thousand francs a year. It would be like old times. Wouldn't you like to share a room with your Léonie again?"

The reply, when it finally came, was uncompromising.

"No," Ariane said flatly, shuffling the papers she had been examining back into a heavy manila envelope. She glanced up at the corner of it and wondered briefly what the number 63821-III referred to.

"Ariane!"

"Well, I don't want to hurt your feelings, Léonie, but I'd rather have my room to myself. For that matter, I wish you'd knock at the door before you bounce in the way you just did."

"Oh, how *can* you—how can you talk to me like that? After all I've done for you!"

"Done for me!" Ariane echoed. "What have you done for me? All you did was kill my husband."

Léonie's face went white and she became very still.

"What did you say?" she finally whispered.

"Oh, I know you didn't realize what you were doing. But I told you over and over again not to let George have all that rich food—to serve him the things on the diets Dr. LeBlanc ordered. About food, George was like an alcoholic who can't resist the bottle. He was a compulsive eater."

"And I suppose that was *my* fault." The color had suddenly flooded back into Léonie's face.

"It was your fault to the extent that, when I occasionally did get George to start to follow a diet, you would suddenly start to talk about some new dish you were trying out and, of course, George would insist on tasting it. The effect was the same as an alcoholic's first drink. I begged and begged him to eat more simply but, with you tempting him all the time, I was helpless. So he died and you killed him. With kindness, perhaps, but the result was the same. Now I'm a widow . . ." And, for the first time since her husband had died, Ariane began to cry.

"Perhaps you can fool other people, or even yourself, but you can't fool me," Léonie said coldly. "It's no use your pretending to me that you're sorry that gross creature who was your husband is dead. You loathed him!"

Ariane's tears suddenly stopped and she stared at her friend.

"I didn't loath him," she said slowly. "It was you who hated him. Don't think I didn't sense it for all your 'spoiling' him—in fact, that's why I've sometimes wondered . . ." her voice trailed off. "George was good to me and I was grateful. He was good to you, too."

"Good to me?" Léonie exclaimed. "What do you mean, good to me? I worked my fingers to the bone for him—for you both. Why do people from all over the world come here? Because of the restaurant *I* created. But *now,* you're the boss—*now* you're rich! Now that you have everything you want you feel you can kick me away."

"Oh, Léonie, you know that's not true! Of course I realize how much the success of this place is due to you. But, on the other hand, aren't you doing just what you always longed to do? Don't you enjoy what you're doing?"

Léonie didn't answer and Ariane went on. "It's not a question of my kicking you away, Léonie. It's just that I want to lead my own life."

"What do you mean by 'leading your own life'?"

"Just that. Even in the few days since George died, you've been trying to run me . . . where have I been, where am I going, what am I going to do, why don't I do this, why don't I do that? I don't like it!"

"Ariane!" Léonie said beseechingly. "How can you be so cruel! I've always loved you, protected you, helped you ever since we met all those years ago. You were almost a child when I first saw you on the train, a frightened child. And now you talk to me as though I were your enemy. You'll never know all that I have done for you!" Tears began to stream down the older woman's cheeks. "And there is nothing that I *wouldn't* do for you."

"Léonie!" Ariane sighed. "The trouble is that I don't want you to do anything for me. Can't you realize that I'm an adult and want to be left alone?"

"You mean you want me to go?"

"Of course not, Léonie! You know I couldn't run this place without you. But why can't we live here and run our business without interfering with each other?"

"So all you want of me is to be your servant!"

"Léonie, you know perfectly well that you are not a servant! You run everything. Why do you have to be so difficult? I'm tired and I have a headache." Going into the bathroom, Ariane took two aspirins and drank some water. When she came back, Léonie was lying on the bed that had been George's, sobbing. Ariane gave a sigh. Going over to her old friend, she sat down beside her and stroked the head buried in the pillow.

Two hours later, exhausted, she gave in, and it was agreed that the next day Léonie would move her things to Ariane's room.

George Simpson was buried two days later.

CHAPTER XII

Dr. Yves LeBlanc lived in a three-hundred-year-old modernized stone cottage, almost indistinguishable from the granite cliff on which it was perched. It was a three-level affair with a room extending into a tiny rock garden at each level. At the top the rock garden, even in winter a riot of color, circled the house and offered a 360° view. Here, whenever weather permitted, Dr. LeBlanc took his meals and spent whatever leisure he had.

It was a stormy day shortly after George Simpson's funeral, and Annick, the doctor's maid, set the table for his breakfast in the kitchen by the window, from which he could watch the giant waves crashing on the rocks below.

"Madame Ariane looked beautiful in black," she commented, pouring the frothing milk and the coffee into a pint-size cup.

"Yes," the doctor replied, helping himself to a croissant, still warm from the oven.

"When will you be marrying her?" the maid continued, placing a dish of butter on the table.

"Annick!" the doctor thundered, laying down his croissant.

"It's no good yelling 'Annick' at me," the old woman said. "I've known you since you were born and I only wish I had a franc for every pair of diapers I've pinned on you. I knew you had fallen in love with Madame Ariane even before Anne-Marie began to gossip."

"Who the hell is Anne-Marie?"

"Anne-Marie Ledoux. She runs the Café Ledoux. You remember her. Her husband died last year."

"Certainly I remember her. The most foul-mouthed old bitch I've ever known. Her husband died of acute alcoholism; he drank so much there was never anything left to sell to the customers. And what have you and she found to gossip about?"

The old woman drew herself up.

"I don't gossip. I can't help what people tell me and I thought you should know what was being said."

"And what's that?"

"That you are Madame Ariane's lover."

"Oh, my God," Dr. LeBlanc groaned as he pushed his cup away and drew his hand over his eyes. "How long has this gossip been going on?"

"Since you went to the cinema in Brest with Madame Ariane two months ago while Mr. George was in the hospital."

"And going to the cinema makes me Madame Ariane's lover?"

"It wasn't so much the cinema, Monsieur Yves. But when you drove her back to l'Aber-Wrac'h you stopped in the lay-by and were there for over two hours. And that, of course, is just below the Ledoux cafe. Anne-Marie watched you through her binoculars the whole time."

"Oh, God!" the doctor groaned. "I remember. The cafe was shuttered. It hadn't opened for the season."

"Since her husband died, Anne-Marie lives there all the year round in the back. She always watches what goes on through a crack in the shutters. As you know, couples frequently stop there."

"If Anne-Marie watched closely enough, she would know I was not Madame Ariane's lover," the doctor observed, lighting a cigarette. "At least not on that occasion. But I suppose she assumed there were others."

"Anne-Marie does not always speak the exact truth about what she sees."

"I understand. God! What a silly mess."

"Why don't you marry Madame Ariane? She is such a nice lady and it's time you had a wife. Anyway, I want to hold your son in my arms before I die."

"You can't start talking to a woman about marrying her right after her husband is buried." Just then there was the sound of knocking at the front door, which was upstairs, and Annick went off to open it, grumbling under her breath. She came back a few minutes later, looking troubled.

"There is a policeman upstairs who wants to see you. I've put him in your study."

"Did he say what he wanted?"

"No, just that he wanted to talk to you. I think he's from Brest."

Dr. LeBlanc shrugged, stubbed out his cigarette and went up to his study.

A tall man, who appeared to be in the early thirties, was standing by the window watching the turbulent sea at the foot of the cliff. He turned as the doctor came into the room.

"Dr. LeBlanc?" he asked.

"Yes, I am Dr. LeBlanc."

"You have a magnificent view," the policeman said. "It must be hard for you to tear yourself away."

"Sometimes it is, particularly on stormy days."

"I'm the Commissaire Verdier, from Brest. I've come to see you about the death of"—he glanced at a notebook in his hand—"an American gentleman, Monsieur George Simpson. I believe you were the attending physician and signed the death certificate?"

"Yes, that is correct."

"You gave the cause of death as an acute attack of gastritis?"

"Yes."

"What made you think this was what caused Mr. Simpson's death?"

"I have been attending Mr. Simpson for several years and during all this time he has suffered from gastric disturbances, chiefly caused by massive overeating. The last few months these upsets became much more frequent and more violent. Two months ago I put him in the hospital in Brest for tests and a gastroscopic examination. They revealed nothing but bad inflammation. Mr. Simpson was also very overweight. Presumably the constant strain on his heart was finally too much. The attacks he had recently, as I said, had become more and more severe and even entailed mental confusion, prostration, and, on one occasion, coma."

"Tell me, Doctor, did you expect Mr. Simpson's death?"

Dr. LeBlanc hesitated.

"I'm bound to say that I did not. He had come through so many even more severe attacks I assumed, wrongly, as it turned out, that he would do so again."

"So that his death was a surprise to you?"

"In a way, yes. I had no reason to suspect that his heart was in poor condition in spite of his weight. The electrocardiogram I had taken showed nothing. May I ask the reason for these questions?"

"We had reason to believe that Mr. Simpson's death was due to something more than a gastric disturbance. His body has been exhumed and an autopsy performed."

Dr. LeBlanc felt himself go pale under his tan.

"With what result?" he asked.

"The death was caused by a massive dose of digitalis—far more than would have been required even if he had had heart trouble."

"Digitalis!"

"Did you prescribe digitalis?"

"Never. As I said, so far as I was aware, there was nothing wrong with his heart."

"But you have the drug in your possession."

"Of course; most doctors do. It's a very useful one."

"You gave none to Mr. Simpson?"

"No." There was a slight pause. "What is it you suspect?" he finally asked. "Suicide? Murder?"

"We suspect nothing. We are making inquiries. You have no plans to leave l'Aber-Wrac'h in the immediate future?"

"None." The doctor hesitated. "What made you suspect that Mr. Simpson did not die a natural death?" he asked.

"Certain information we received."

"I see! And I think I know where your 'information' came from. Well, I expect I shall be seeing you again soon."

After the police had gone, Dr. LeBlanc stood a long time

looking at the storm. Then he moved over to the telephone and started to pick it up, then changed his mind.

"What did they want?" Annick asked, standing at the door.

"Your friend Anne-Marie has done her work well. As far as I can figure out, they wanted to talk to me because they think I murdered Mr. George."

"Monsieur Yves, you shouldn't make such jokes."

The doctor took off his shoes and pulled on his fishing boots.

"It's unfortunately no joke. They probably think it was either I or Madame Ariane or possibly both of us."

"But Mr. George died of a stomach illness. You said so yourself."

"They don't think I was telling the truth. So Mr. George's body has been dug up for examination." And the doctor, slipping on a fisherman's raincoat and a sou'wester, opened the door and went out into the storm to start his rounds.

* * *

Madame Ariane, the day after her husband's funeral, insisted on resuming her duties.

"Why don't you wait a few days?" Letitia asked when she came to relieve her at the reception desk. "You must be terribly tired."

"I'm tired but it is not a physical fatigue. I'll be better off with something to keep me busy. And you've been shut up in the hotel too long. Go for a nice walk, my dear, and get some fresh air."

It had stormed all morning, but the worst was over when Letitia, dressed for wet weather, left the inn. The wind was still high and the sea turbulent and she knew of a place a few miles from l'Aber-Wrac'h where the view, when the waves were high, was spectacular. Letitia decided that a long, brisk walk was just what she needed.

Ken McCabe was coming out of the tobacconist's when she went by and he fell into step beside her.

"Going anywhere special?" he asked.

"Just for a walk."

"Mind if I tag along?"

"Not at all. But I'm not feeling very talkative."

"Silent companionship is very restful."

They walked on for ten minutes without speaking.

"I'd better warn you that I'm going for quite a long walk," Letitia finally said. "There and back is about nine miles."

"Suits me."

"Don't you care where you're going?"

"Nope. I'm just killing time."

Letitia said nothing for a few minutes.

"You know, I hate that expression—'killing time'!" she finally said. "We have so little I don't ever intend to 'kill' any. I want to live every minute I can. Even when things are bad and, of course, from time to time they are bound to be, I want to feel it all.

> We are awake so little on this earth
> And we shall sleep so long
> And lie so late
> If there is any knocking at that gate
> Which is the gate of death, the gate of birth."

"Did you write that?" Ken asked with interest.

"I wish I had. It's from a poem called 'Credo'; I don't remember who wrote it. But I like it."

"I won't talk about 'killing time' again. I didn't really mean it, anyway. The present moment is most pleasurable."

They continued on in silence.

"The trouble is that I *do* have a feeling that you are here in Brittany more or less 'killing time'—that you're waiting for something. You seem a most unlikely person to be staying at the Auberge."

"Why do you say that?"

"I don't quite know." Letitia was troubled as she glanced at him. "You're obviously not a tourist—your car has French license plates. You haven't come for the food—the waitress told me you hardly eat anything even when you have a meal in the restaurant, and most of the time you don't. You don't look as though you were recovering from an illness. You look very healthy in spite of the fact that you're thin. Anyway, it's a wiry thinness. And you don't go sailing, which is another reason people come here."

"About the food, I realize that it's marvelous, but there's too much of it. I can't take all that rich stuff every day. Anyway, if I got into the habit of eating the sort of meal served at the Auberge, it would spoil me for prunes. As for going sailing, I come from North Dakota; the only kind of ships they ever had out there were prairie schooners. And as for recovering from an illness, I've been doing just that—if you can call it an illness."

"What was wrong with you?"

"I stopped three bullets, if you really want to know."

"Bullets!" Letitia exclaimed. "Were you in Vietnam?"

"I was not. Korea briefly, yes. Vietnam, no. Anyway, shooting at people is not a sport restricted to the Far East. It's practiced in Paris, too, though on a more modest scale."

"What on earth were you doing to make someone shoot at you?"

"I was trying to keep an eye on a guy and he didn't like it."

"Are you a detective?"

"Nope. I was in the narcotics racket, but I got out."

"Narcotics racket? Do you mean to tell me you smuggled dope?"

"Look, dope smugglers don't go around talking about their work to comparative strangers, no matter how charming they are. I was a narcotics agent—a clean-living, upright American boy, on the side of mother, flag, and country—or whatever."

"Why did you get out?"

"Well, one gets a little tired of being a clean-living, upright American boy, etc."

"So what do you do now for a living?"

"Right now, I'm 'resting,' as thespians say when they're out of a job."

"L'Aber-Wrac'h doesn't seem exactly an ideal spot for an American to be job-hunting," Letitia remarked after a few minutes.

"I'm not exactly job-hunting. Anyway, after all, *you've* got a job here."

"Not a paid one. It's not the place to find a fortune."

"Unfortunately, I'm beginning to think you may be right." Ken laughed. "But I can always hope, can't I?"

Letitia darted her companion a quick glance from narrowed eyes and they walked on in silence.

"Here we are," she finally said, walking to the stone parapet at the edge of a cliff.

Below an unleashed sea, like a gigantic maddened animal, was hurling itself against the rocks, white foam swirling back as a wave retreated to fling itself forward again with even greater fury, throwing up its spray to the two enthralled spectators above. The rain had stopped but the wind was howling, and when Letitia tried to speak her voice could not be heard over the roar of the crashing sea.

For over half an hour they stood watching the magnificent scene, unable to tear themselves away. Finally, realizing that it would begin to get dark and shivering with cold, they turned reluctantly away and started back to l'Aber-Wrac'h.

"The fascination of Brittany! Wasn't that wonderful?" Letitia exclaimed when they got far enough from the sea to be able to talk without yelling. The wind and cold had whipped color into her cheeks, her golden hair was an unruly mop and her eyes were shining.

"You're beautiful when you're excited," Ken said, looking at her with unconcealed admiration.

"Don't be silly! But it *was* thrilling, wasn't it?"

"It was indeed. And now I'm frozen. Let's stop and have something hot to drink at the next cafe. I see one ahead . . . 'A la Vieille Bretagne.' "

This turned out to be a misnomer. The zinc bar, scoured oak tables, and carved wooden chairs they had expected were replaced by formica, plastics, metal tubes, and neon. The owner, a corpulent man in a blue smock and apron, wearing sabots, seemed an anachronism. He was also obviously proud of his modernity.

"*C'est beau, hein?*" he said complacently, seeing the two customers glance around. "It was finished last week!"

Letitia politely agreed that it was "*beau*" and they ordered coffee.

"One advantage of this hideous modernity," Letitia said, "is that that gleaming espresso coffee machine produces a better drink than the old metal drip things they used to put over individual cups. By the time the water had worked its way through, the resulting brew was stone-cold. If you tried to hurry things along by jiggling the insides, the sole result was blistered fingers. I never understood how the metal could be so hot and the coffee so not."

"Would you like a drop of cognac in your coffee?"

"I don't believe so, thanks. Now that I'm out of the wind I'm quite warm."

"May I ask one favor of you?" Ken said, stirring his coffee.

"What is that?"

"I'd like you to look at a couple of photographs."

Letitia looked at her companion questioningly.

"They are photographs of a man. I should like you to tell me whether you recognize him."

Letitia looked troubled.

"I wouldn't want to do anyone any harm," she said.

"It couldn't possibly do anyone any harm."

"Well, if you're sure . . ."

"Quite sure." And Ken drew two photographs of George Zillitch out of his pocket.

Letitia examined them closely.

"Well?" Ken finally asked.

She handed the pictures back to him.

"If you were to tell me that these were pictures of Mr. Simpson, taken years ago, I would be prepared to believe you. But I don't recognize him. It might be him or it might not."

"That's about what I expected you to say," Ken replied with a sigh, pocketing the photographs.

The walk back to the Auberge was, for the most part, a silent one, each busy with private thoughts.

"You know, I feel as though I'm living in a sort of state of suspended animation, waiting for something to happen—something evil. If you suspect that Mr. Simpson sold narcotics or something like that, you're barking up the wrong tree. Mr. Simpson was much too—oh, I suppose the word would be 'inert'—to do anything like that," Letitia said as they neared the inn.

"I don't suspect Mr. Simpson of being a drug dealer. Anyway, even if he had been, it would have nothing to do with me. As I told you, I'm no longer concerned."

"That's what you say. I'm certain, though, that it was because of Mr. Simpson that you came here. Can't I know what this is all about?"

Ken's attention was caught by a small blue police car parked in front of the village pharmacy. As they walked past it the driver, alone in the car, watched them with expressionless eyes.

"Am I right?" Letitia persisted. "Aren't you here because of Mr. Simpson?"

"Yes."

"*Please* tell me what it's all about!"

"Grist for your literary mill?" he grinned.

"Chiefly wild curiosity," Letitia answered. "Do tell me!"

Ken sighed.

"I wish I knew it all myself. I'll tell you if and when I can."

For days, Ken had restlessly waited word from Jean Labruyère and had finally called him. But Jean had no news.

"I'll let you know as soon as I hear anything, Ken," Jean assured him. "The glass has been examined but the laboratory refuses to tell my cousin what the results are at the present time. He has the impression that something unexpected has been discovered."

"But all I wanted was an official identification of the fingerprint."

"I know. But I think an analysis of the liquid left in the glass was made with some surprising results. I'll get in touch with you as soon as I can, I promise you."

But he had heard nothing further.

Ariane smiled at the windblown couple as they came in.

"You look as though you had had a good walk. Your cheeks are quite red." She turned to Ken. "There have been several telephone calls for you, Mr. McCabe," she went on. "Whoever it was said he would call back." Just then the phone rang and she turned to answer it.

"Oui. Un moment, s'il vous plaît. Je vous le passe. This is the telephone call for you," she said to Ken. "Do you want to take it in the booth?"

"Ken?" Jean's voice asked. "I finally had a call from my cousin. You are right about the fingerprint. Your Simpson and Zillitch are one and the same man. But it seems that he did not die a natural death. The police suspect he may have been murdered."

"Murdered! What are you talking about?"

"The remnants of the orange juice or whatever it was were analyzed and enough digitalis was found to kill a couple of men. You really stumbled onto something."

"But, Jean, that's ridiculous. The man has been sick for months."

"Yes, well then perhaps he got tired of being sick and killed himself."

"For God's sake! This is incredible!"

"It may be incredible but that is the situation. I thought I'd better tell you as soon as possible."

"Oh, God! Well, I expect that blows my projects sky-high. While he was alive, I figured I might be able to scare him into giving back some of the loot, or its equivalent. But now . . . What will the Brest police do now?"

"I don't know," Jean replied. "I expect they'll do a little quiet investigating."

"Thanks, Jean. Let me know if you hear anything more."

And Ken slowly replaced the receiver.

CHAPTER XIII

Brittany is at its most beautiful after a storm, and Letitia found she had thrown off the oppressive feeling of impending trouble of the evening before and was light-hearted when she got up the next morning to see that the sun was out; little fleecy clouds scudding along merely emphasized the blue of the sky and from her window she could see white horses capping the dark-blue waves. The air was still brisk and she decided to skip breakfast to fit a morning walk in before taking up her duties at the reception desk at nine o'clock.

cop. 2

There were only a half dozen guests staying at the inn so that it took her very little time to post the previous day's charges in the ledger, and the mail, when it came, was scanty. There were three letters for Ken McCabe, however, two typed and one written in what looked like a woman's hand—a woman with a strong character, Letitia decided, examining the firm, heavy strokes of the pen. It was postmarked New York; there was no address of sender and Letitia was angry with herself for her interest in it and also for feeling a tiny stab of jealousy. She quickly turned to distribute the mail in the proper pigeonholes.

She turned back to see Mademoiselle Léonie, her face like thunder, stride past the desk without speaking, a large basket on her arm. Unlike Madame Ariane, Mademoiselle Léonie was always cold to the staff. But she usually did at least nod a good morning, and Letitia briefly wondered what had upset her. The fishing boats, she decided, had probably been delayed by the storm; from the window she could see that they were only now coming into the little harbor. They were usually there before breakfast and Mademoiselle Léonie was always on hand at their arrival to have first pick of the fish that would be served at the Auberge that day.

Shortly afterwards, Madame Ariane came up to check what reservations had come in through the mail. She was pale and her reddened eyes looked as though she had been crying.

"Only one reservation," Letitia said in answer to her question. "Maître Besnard has written to say he is coming on Friday to spend the weekend and wants his usual suite."

"He must have an important case coming up," Madame Ariane said, with a tired smile. "He always likes number thirteen—he says it's a good-luck charm for him. Whenever he has spent a weekend in number thirteen he has always won his pending case. I tell him it's probably because he's had complete quiet and plenty of rest and good food, but he insists it's suite thirteen."

Letitia noted the dark circles under Madame Ariane's eyes and realized that she had lost a good deal of weight over the last two weeks.

"You don't look well," Letitia said, concerned. "Don't you think you should get away for a week or two? You've gone through such a bad time lately, you need a rest."

"Perhaps later. I can't get away right now," Ariane replied. "If anyone wants me, I'll be in the linen room," she added abruptly.

"Goodness! Everybody seems to be out of sorts today," Letitia said to herself as she turned to answer the telephone.

One of Ariane's responsibilities was to keep the Auberge's linen supplies in order, and, leaving Letitia, she made her way to the only "office" she had, which was the linen room. Shutting the door, she sank down in the chair behind the rickety old desk and rested her aching head on her folded arms. Her mind went back to the night before and she realized that, whatever else she owed her late husband, her chief debt to him was due to the fact that he had stood between her and Léonie. During the years of her marriage she had at least been spared the scenes to which her friend had all too often subjected her when they had shared the little studio; Ariane had even more or less forgotten about them. The previous night's performance, however, had equaled and even surpassed any that had occurred in earlier years.

What a fool I was to let her talk me into sharing a room with her again, she thought. What I'll do is go away for a while— but, oh, God! She'll probably want to come with me. And even if she doesn't, what will it be like when I return?

And she sighed as she got up and began arranging the piles of linen. She was checking an inventory of sheets when there was a knock at the door. She opened it to a stranger.

"Commissaire Verdier," he announced himself holding out a metal identification disk for her inspection. "The young lady at the desk told me I would find you here."

"What can I do for you?" Ariane asked, standing in the doorway.

"May I come in? I have one or two questions I'd like to ask you about your late husband."

Reluctantly Ariane opened the door to the policeman and indicated a chair while she sat down at her desk.

"Questions about my husband? What did you want to know?"

The commissaire took a notebook out of his pocket and glanced at it as though refreshing his memory. Then he fixed dark eyes, set in a long pale face, on the woman in front of him. There was a short silence before he spoke.

"How long were you married to Mr. Simpson?"

"Just a little over five years."

"What can you tell me about his background?"

"His background? What did you want to know?"

"Where he was born, who his people were, what he did before he came to France . . ."

Ariane frowned as she thought back.

"He was born in the United States . . . I think somewhere in Massa—Mass-a-chusetts," she brought the name out with some difficulty. "After he had finished school he went into the hotel business. Then the war came and he joined the Army. When it was over, he settled down in France."

"What was his father's profession?"

"It seems to me George said he had a shop."

"What kind of a shop?"

"I'm not sure, but I think a food shop."

"Where are his parents now?"

"They died during the war."

"You never went to the United States with him to meet his family?"

"I never went to the United States and, anyway, he told me he had no family."

"The mother and father who died, they were rich?"

Ariane looked surprised.

"Oh, no. He went to work when he was sixteen, I think."

"But Mr. Simpson was a man of considerable means, wasn't he?"

"Yes, he was. He was always very generous to me and it was his money that created the Auberge."

"If his people were poor where did this wealth come from?"

"He never said anything about that. I supposed he earned it in the hotel business."

"But he could not have been in the hotel business very long before the war came."

"I remember he told me he and a partner owned a factory after the war, too."

"Where?"

"Here in France."

"What sort of factory?"

Ariane thought back. "He only mentioned it once," she said, "and I can't really remember. I think, though, they must have made some kind of dolls. I seem to recollect that it was called La Poupée."

"What happened to it?"

"He told me he sold his share to his partner."

"When was this?"

"It must have been about eight years ago."

"You think this factory and the hotel business were the sources of his money?"

"I don't really know where his money came from. He never

told me and, as it was not any of my business, I never asked him."

"How did you meet Mr. Simpson?" M. Verdier asked, after a pause.

The color flooded into Ariane's face and she made no answer.

"Well?" the policeman asked.

"That is a personal matter I prefer not to discuss."

The commissaire did not insist.

"The inn is in your name, I believe."

"Yes. George wanted it that way."

"What happened to the income from it?"

"What do you mean, what happened to it?"

"The Auberge has been making a profit, hasn't it?"

"Yes."

"What did you do with the money?"

"We used what we needed and whatever was left of George's and my share went into my bank account."

"*Your* bank account? Or a joint account?"

"My bank account. There was no joint account."

"What about your husband's account?"

"As far as I know, since we have been here, he has had none."

"A wealthy man with no bank account? How did he pay for things?"

"In cash."

"Where did he get the cash?"

"I told you. From the receipts. For the most part, our clients pay in cash. We have a good deal of liquid money in the safe. Sometimes it has worried me."

There was a pause.

"You mentioned you and your husband's share of the profits of the Auberge. Who got the other shares?"

"My husband and I got two thirds of the income. The other third goes to Mademoiselle Lafauve."

"One third of the capital investment came from her?"

"No, she provided no capital. But it is due to her hard work and brilliance, even genius, as a cook that the Auberge has been so successful. It was only right that she should share in the profits."

"Will this arrangement, that you receive two thirds of the profits and Mademoiselle Lafauve one third, continue?"

"I suppose so. I had not thought about it."

"What about your husband's will?"

"I don't believe he made one. I have looked through his papers and didn't find one. And, since the Auberge is in my name, there was really no need for a will."

"Assuming he had no other assets to leave."

"Yes, assuming that."

"Even with just the Auberge, you are, then, a wealthy widow." There was an emphasis on the next to the last word that caused Ariane to frown.

"Please tell me what this is about . . . why you are asking all these questions."

But the policeman made no direct reply.

"Did your husband have any enemies?"

"Of course not. My husband led a very quiet life. He didn't mix with the hotel guests and had no real friends in France and certainly no enemies. He spoke French very badly and, also, he was a man who liked his privacy."

"Still, he did know some people. Those who worked in the hotel, for instance."

"He knew them, of course, and occasionally spoke to them. But, outside of giving instructions on how to perform certain tasks, he didn't talk to them much."

"What kind of instructions?"

Ariane thought for a moment. "Well, the last I can remember was to the maids. He told them to stack the linen in the order in which it is used, when making the beds, and then finish one side completely before moving to the other side. That way they could make a bed in less than three minutes, whereas the old way it used to take them nearly double that. He rarely gave instructions himself, though—it was usually through me."

"What about Mademoiselle Lafauve?"

"That was different. She was a partner. We discussed everything with her."

"Did your husband and she get along together?"

"Oh, certainly." The barely perceptible hesitation before Ariane's reply did not go unnoticed by the policeman.

"What about Dr. LeBlanc? That is someone else your husband must have known fairly well."

"Well, naturally. It was Dr. LeBlanc who took care of him through his illnesses."

"Quite unsuccessfully, it would seem."

"Unsuccessfully?"

"Your husband died, didn't he?" There was a long pause. "Tell me, Madame Simpson, are you Dr. LeBlanc's mistress?" M. Verdier inquired conversationally.

Ariane stared at the policeman and turned pale.

"Am I what?" she finally whispered.

"Dr. LeBlanc's mistress," M. Verdier repeated equably.

"Can you come into my house and ask me questions of that sort and not give me any explanation as to why you ask them?" Ariane finally asked, her voice trembling.

"In point of fact, I can. However, I will tell you that we have exhumed the body of your late husband."

Ariane looked uncomprehending.

"Exhumed George's body? But why?"

"We had reason to suspect that his death was not a natural one. As it has turned out, we were right."

"But that's ridiculous! Of course he died a natural death. Dr. LeBlanc can tell you; he took care of him for—" Suddenly Ariane stopped as she began to understand the full import of what had gone before. "But it's absurd," she cried. "I was with George, right to the end."

"Alone with him," the commissaire said meaningfully.

Ariane looked stunned.

"I see," she finally said with dignity. "You think I killed my husband. I didn't, of course, but it seems to me that the best thing I can do now is consult a lawyer."

"That is as you wish. For my part, I am merely investigating your husband's death and, naturally, must take into consideration all possibilities, including that of suicide."

"That is a possibility you need not bother about. My husband certainly did not kill himself. He was not that kind of man."

"All sorts and conditions of men commit suicide."

"Not George. He was not a man of emotions. Not everyone would have enjoyed the vegetable sort of existence he led, but he did; he enjoyed it thoroughly."

"Even his illnesses? Many people kill themselves because they think they have an incurable disease."

"George didn't think he had an incurable disease. He knew perfectly well what was wrong with him. It's hard to explain it to you but he was not really ill at all—even though he died. What he had were stomach upsets . . . they were painful while they lasted but as soon as they had passed he was perfectly well again. Every time he went to Vichy or Baden-Baden or one of the spas, he came back cured. But he lived to eat; as soon as he returned, the whole dreary business started up again. It was like an alcoholic and his bottle, except that I think George had more fun." Ariane shrugged. "In a sense, of course, he *did* commit suicide, but not in the way you mean."

"Tell me about the night he died in as much detail as you can remember."

Ariane buried her face in her hands for a moment while she collected her thoughts. Then, facing the commissaire, she told the story. The policeman listened attentively, making notes as she talked.

"When you gave him his orangeade, did you add any medicine to it? Something to make him sleep, for instance?"

"I didn't add anything."

"Please try to think carefully. Could he himself have slipped something into the drink?"

"Not possibly. I held the glass to his lips but he pushed my hand away and said he preferred to hold it himself."

"Then what did you do?"

"I let him hold it."

"And then?"

"I took the cup of tea Mademoiselle Lafauve had made for me off the tray, sat down on the chair beside the bed, and started to drink it."

"Where had you placed the tray?"

"On the dresser."

"When you picked up the cup, did you turn your back to the bed?"

"Only long enough to put some sugar in the tea."

"But you did have your back to the bed briefly."

"Not for more than ten seconds, I would think."

"Did your husband comment on the orangeade . . . did he mention its being bitter or anything like that?"

"I asked him if it was all right and he said that it was wet and cold and that was all he wanted."

"I suppose Dr. LeBlanc did prescribe medicines for your husband?"

"Yes, but George took none that night. He didn't really believe much in medicines . . . he took them when he was feeling ill but as soon as he began to feel better he took no more. He said nature could do the rest of the work. And the night he died he seemed to be feeling so very much better."

"You don't know what medicines Dr. LeBlanc prescribed?"

"No. The prescriptions were sent to the pharmacy and I followed the instructions. Dr. LeBlanc or the pharmacy will be able to tell you what the medicines were."

"About your relations with Dr. LeBlanc—"

Ariane stood up.

"I had no what you call 'relations' with Dr. LeBlanc. What makes you think I did? He was strictly my husband's doctor."

"You and Dr. LeBlanc were observed seated in his car, which was parked in front of the Café Ledoux. You were there together for over two hours and, according to our information, the doctor was making love to you and you seemed not to object. Do you consider that this agrees with your statement that he was 'strictly your husband's doctor and nothing else'?"

Ariane turned white.

"I have nothing more to say," she finally answered from between stiff lips. "If you wish to arrest me, go ahead. I did not murder my husband. I am not nor have I ever been Dr. LeBlanc's mistress."

"But you admit to having spent about two hours in his arms?"

"I admit nothing; I deny nothing."

"One other question and then I'll leave you. What happens to your money—to the Auberge—should you die?"

Ariane looked startled.

"I don't know," she said.

"You have never made a will?"

"No."

"Your husband never suggested you make a will in his favor?"

"We never talked about wills. Anyway, if I died before he did, wouldn't he have inherited everything automatically?"

"Have you no family?"

"No. I was a foundling. I was brought up in an orphanage."

"In that case, your husband would have inherited from you. But the situation is different now."

"Yes. I suppose I should make a will as soon as possible."

"In whose favor?"

"Oh, Mademoiselle Lafauve, of course."

"Well, thank you very much. I'll probably want to talk to you again soon."

After the commissaire had gone Ariane sat a long time staring into space. Then she glanced at her watch; it was a quarter to one. Suddenly making up her mind, she hurried down the corridor to her room and, sitting down on the bed beside the telephone, she quickly dialed a number.

"Yves, it's Ariane," she said in answer to a gruff "hello." "I've got to talk to you. The police have been here. About George. They think I killed him."

"Ariane, you shouldn't have called me. They've been here, too. Both our telephones are probably tapped."

"Oh, God! Somebody saw us that day in your car."

"It seems that it's been local gossip for weeks, now. That bitch, Madame Ledoux who runs the Café Ledoux, had a happy after-

noon watching us through her binoculars and spread the glad
word throughout l'Aber-Wrac'h."

"Yves, what'll we do? Can't I see you? There are so many
questions I want to ask you. Couldn't I slip out to meet you
somewhere?"

There was a short silence.

"I want to see you very much but an attempt at a secret meeting would be the height of folly. If we meet, it must be done
openly."

"Can you come here, then?"

"Ariane, how much do you care about what people say?"

"What do you mean?"

"Would it make you very unhappy to be the subject of gossip?"

"Whether it makes me unhappy or not isn't going to change
the fact that I *am* the subject of gossip. Why do you ask?"

"Because I should like to tell the police the truth—that you
are not my mistress but that I'm very much in love with you and
that I hope you love me."

"Yves!"

"Well! I am in love with you, as you know."

"But won't that give them just what they want . . . a motive?"

"They already have that, or they think they do. We'll just
tell them we plan to get married after a suitable lapse of time.
I can't see we'll be any worse off. I'll come over to the Auberge
as soon as I've finished my rounds this afternoon—probably
around five o'clock. Meanwhile, I'm very much afraid you may
be going to need a good lawyer. Do you know one?"

"I don't know any lawyers, good or bad. I've never had anything to do with them. Oh, wait a moment. I *do* know one. And
he's very good, or at least very famous. Maître Besnard. He
comes here for a weekend about every three months and I know
that he is coming tonight. He has always been very friendly. We
can consult him."

"Maître Besnard? Splendid. You'd better talk to him as soon as
possible. Bear in mind that in a day or so this will probably be
splashed all over the front pages of newspapers and, temporarily
at least, the Auberge won't have many guests."

"Right now, that is the least of my worries. But there is one question I must ask you, Yves. Are the police right? Were you wrong about George's death?"

"I was wrong," Dr. LeBlanc said heavily.

"What did kill him?"

"Didn't the police tell you?"

"No."

"He died of an overdose of digitalis."

"Was that a medicine you prescribed?"

"No. It's a heart medicine and there appeared to be nothing wrong with your husband's heart. I prescribed things for his stomach. But, of course, I have plenty of digitalis on hand. The whole thing is very difficult and very strange. We'll talk about it later. Meanwhile, don't forget that I love you and that we're going to lick this. Goodbye."

"Goodbye, my darling."

After hanging up, Ariane sat beside the phone for some time, lost in thought. Then, with a sigh, she got up and left the room. After she had been gone a few minutes, the door of the bathroom, which had been ajar, opened and Léonie Lafauve came out. Her face was white and her beady black eyes had an odd expression in them. She seemed strangely excited.

CHAPTER XIV

Commissaire Verdier, of the Brest police, was elegantly tall and looked as though he would be more at home on a tennis court than in a police station. In point of fact, he was a fine tennis player but he was as clear-eyed in observing the scene of a crime and those suspected of it as he was in gauging the speed and trajectory of an oncoming tennis ball.

Jacques Verdier's father had taken what, in France, is the gigantic step from peasant to well-to-do bourgeois in one generation. Owner of a small vineyard, he had fallen very much in love with a young schoolteacher, the daughter of a postman, and, despite her reluctance to marry a peasant, she finally succumbed to his good looks and obvious adoration. In the first year of their marriage, disaster struck. A cold, wet summer completely ruined his grape harvest and the wine turned out to be undrinkable. Desperate for money, he remembered that his grandmother had made her own special aromatic vinegar, which neighbors were delighted to be permitted to buy. He dug out her old recipe and, with his young wife's help, turned his year's wine into vinegar and proceeded to try to market it. He succeeded through a combination of luck and perseverance and soon was running a very profitable small factory the output of which was sold exclusively to high-class restaurants. In fact, for a restaurant to be permitted to buy Verdier vinegar was a status symbol mentioned on the menu. M. Verdier and his family continued to live simply, and the profits of the business were used to buy up farms and other real estate, which all proved to be excellent investments.

Intensely proud of his good-looking only son, he decided, when Jacques was fourteen, that he was to be the one who would pull the family much further up the social ladder and become a gentleman. With this in view, M. Verdier moved into a comfortable home in a nearby town close to his factory and saw to it that the boy had all the advantages that money could buy and, later on, insisted that he study law. While he expected Jacques ultimately to take over his financial interests, a legal career for a few years would, he felt, add immeasurably to the family prestige and perhaps open the way to a future in politics. M. Verdier even permitted himself to dream of a day when his son might be in the Elysée.

It was, therefore, first with incredulity and then with outrage that M. Verdier greeted his son's calm announcement, after he had finished his law studies, that he was going into police work.

"I'll disinherit you!" M. Verdier spluttered. "Every penny of my money will go to your sister!"

"I'm a lawyer, remember?" Jacques grinned. "Under French law, you can't disinherit any of your children even if they displease you. It's share and share alike and you know it as well as I do."

"A *flic!* Better to be a criminal—it's more profitable."

"But not a particularly relaxing existence. One would always be worrying—at least, I should; prisons here are old, decrepit, and damnably uncomfortable—no hot and cold running water, and a bucket for you-know-what. I should hate this."

"But why not law? It's a fine career!"

"Father, I've never been more agonizingly bored in my life than during this past year in a law office. You can't *imagine* what it's like."

"Come into the factory, then."

"What would *you* do? You're only fifty-two and you've never been sick a day in your life. Do you want to spend the rest of it contemplating your navel? You, with all your energy? Nonsense! And there's no room for two of us. Anyway, I'm not much more interested in the manufacture of vinegar than I am in the legal profession. No, Father, you marry Bettine off to a nice young man who likes vinegar and you can have a happy time teaching him all you know and browbeating him for the next thirty years, poor devil!"

"Your sister is not yet twelve," M. Verdier pointed out.

"She'll get older," his son assured him. "They always do."

"But why the police? There are other things. You can go into a business—firms like Pechiney, Creusot-Schneider, Dassault—they all employ lawyers."

Jacques Verdier walked about the room, jiggling the change in his pocket.

"Yes, and these lawyers spend days, weeks, and years checking the fine print on contracts. No thank you. I want to struggle against something—pit myself against an enemy. In earlier times I should probably have joined the army to fight in faraway places. Now there are not outlets for the aggressions normal for the male animal of my age. I can, of course, be a public menace behind the steering wheel of a car, as most of my peers are, or I can become a revolutionary and blow up airplanes and so forth and fight policemen. Or I can fight criminals, which, to me, makes more sense. Anyway, Father, I'm not selling myself into slavery. If, at the end of a few years, I find this is not for me, I can always resign."

"Then you'll be too old to start all over again," the father grumbled.

But Jacques Verdier had his own way and went off to spend his year in the ancient Ursuline convent, transformed into a police training school, in the mountain fastness of the Mont d'Or, an isolated spot of singular peace and beauty. Here young men who had degrees in law, sciences, or the arts were trained for the upper echelons of police work.

Jacques Verdier did well in his chosen career and, six years after his graduation, he was named *commissaire de police* in Brest. Moreover, he reinstated himself in his father's good graces by marrying a classmate he had met in law school who was the daughter of an up-and-coming cabinet minister. True, the girl's parents, though also of the bourgeoisie, had begun by refusing to countenance such a *mésalliance,* having hoped for the off-spring of a ducal family, who had also courted their pretty daughter, as a son-in-law. The girl, however, by the use of a little judicious blackmail, had quickly brought them around. France, she had pointed out, was supposed to be a democracy, the home of *liberté, égalité, fraternité.* How would it look, she asked, particularly with an election coming up, if, when the press enquired why her marriage was to be such a hole-in-the-corner affair, she were to explain why her father was opposed to it. This device worked admirably and the wedding was a splendid one, honored by the attendance of the President of France and most of his government. M. Verdier *père* was beside himself with joy and even, of his own volition, settled a handsome allowance on the young couple.

Nonetheless Jacques Verdier was a peasant's son who had spent his formative years in a village. Town dwellers, in France, if they give the matter any thought, consider that those who live in the country lead boring, uninteresting lives. It is true that village life is not for the young, eager for something new and different. For the settled and the elderly, though, compared to the burgher, country folk lead lives of constant drama and excitement. For they not only have their own lives, but they participate intimately in that of all their neighbors, and no trained detective's powers of observation is more acute than theirs. A strange car parked in front of a house? In a trice, the countryside knows that the Marsacs' daughter, who had run off with the tractor salesman from the north and given birth to illegitimate twins, has returned to visit her parents, accompanied by her children and also by a real husband, a fairly prosperous widower who needed help to run his grocery store.

The doctor's car in front of Madame Michard's dwelling? They all know she suffers from diabetes so, they decide, her leg must be worse and when, in fact, she is taken to the hospital for its amputation, the whole community rallies around to run her little dry-goods store until, six months later, she returns, on crutches, to run it herself.

Unfortunately, as the commissaire was only too well aware, there are less wholesome aspects of this intimate involvement with other people's lives: gossip is rife and malicious tongues take every opportunity to wag. Insofar as the death of Mr. Simpson was concerned, the commissariat in Brest had received three anonymous letters from l'Aber-Wrac'h, two obviously from the same source, suggesting that the hotel owner's death might bear looking into in view of the relations between his widow and the doctor. And this even before the Sûreté in Paris had advised the commissaire by phone of the results of the analysis of the orangeade and suggested the exhumation of George Simpson's body for the purpose of an autopsy and, should the results warrant, an investigation. He was told that a report from Paris would be put in the mail for him.

The exhumation had taken place, the autopsy had been performed, and, the results having clearly warranted the next step, Jacques Verdier, with the approval of the examining magistrate, Judge Fouillis, had begun his investigation, wondering, since he had not yet received the promised report, how it happened that the Sûreté in Paris had learned of something that had happened in his own bailiwick before he had.

The report was on his desk when he returned from his first visit to the Auberge; he read it through carefully twice, then asked the telephone operator to get him Ken McCabe at the Auberge des Rochers in l'Aber-Wrac'h.

"This is Commissaire Verdier," he said when he heard Ken's voice. "I have just received a report from Paris on the Simpson matter and I think it's about time you and I had a talk."

"I think it is, too," Ken replied. "I've been expecting to hear from you."

"How soon can you come in to Brest?"

"In half an hour."

"Very well. I'll expect you at two thirty."

While he waited for the American, the commissaire sent for his assistant.

"What's happened to Judge Fouillis' search warrant?" he asked. "I asked for it yesterday."

"The judge's office called to say it would be here in half an hour. The judge had to go to the dentist this morning and was out of town attending the wedding of his son earlier in the week. He has only just received your request."

"As soon as it comes, take four men with you to l'Aber-Wrac'h. One should go to Dr. LeBlanc's cottage, talk to his maid, and go through his papers, particularly his prescription duplicates. He should also take possession of the file on George Simpson's illnesses and death. Two of the men should interview the personnel at the inn and any guests who were there at the time of the death. It's unlikely that there will be any—it's a place people stop for a night or two, especially at this time of the year. One man should find out what the village gossips are saying in the cafes, at the butcher's, the baker's, the grocery, etc., particularly with regard to Madame Simpson and the doctor. Tell him to try to find out how much truth there is in this rumor that they are lovers. As for you, I want you to interview Mademoiselle Léonie Lafauve, who runs the dining room of the Auberge. Get her detailed version of what occurred the night of Mr. Simpson's death and, so far as you can, check it. As I understand it, Mr. and Mrs. Simpson had two rooms on the ground floor. I want you to go through them with a fine-tooth comb. Look particularly for medicines and medicine bottles. Look through all papers and documents and bring anything that seems of importance to me here. Madame Simpson has a desk in the linen room; go through that, too."

"But won't most of Mr. Simpson's papers be in English? I don't know any English."

"All right. Bring away anything that is in English. If there is a safe, have that opened as well. Examine the rooms first and leave the papers to the last. Seal up anything you haven't finished by this evening. Perhaps you'd better take an extra man with you to help you. I'll be here all the rest of the afternoon; call me if you find anything of particular interest."

When his assistant had gone, Verdier picked up the phone again.

"Call the Registre de Commerce in Paris and have them give you all available information on a company which was in existence about eight or nine years ago. It was a limited-liability company called La Poupée and one of the owners was a George Simpson. I want to know who the other owners were, what the capital investment was, the address, exactly what they manufactured, everything. Call me when you have the information."

A few moments later, Ken McCabe was ushered into the room. As the two men shook hands, they observed each other and apparently liked what they saw.

"Sit down and tell me what this is all about," the commissaire said. "I have had a report from Paris about it but it is far from clear. How long have you been at l'Aber-Wrac'h?"

"It's been over three weeks now since I arrived."

"Really? I got the impression that you had only been there a few days. You were there before Mr. Simpson's death, in that case. Just how were you concerned with him?"

"It wasn't George Simpson dead that concerned me. I was interested in him alive. His death was, in fact, a bad blow. L'Aber-Wrac'h was the end of a long trail for me. I came to find out whether George Simpson and Major George Zillitch, for whom I had been searching, were one and the same person, as I thought. I had every reason to believe I was right, but, for my purpose, I needed proof—legal proof. Unfortunately, when I got to the Auberge des Rochers, Simpson (or Zillitch) was ill and it was not possible for me even to see him, let alone confront him."

"Who was this Major George Zillitch and why were you looking for him?"

"I'd better tell you the story from the beginning. But I must warn you that it is a lengthy one and, since it concerns events that took place twenty-five years ago, I doubt that it will help you much in your effort to try to find out who killed him."

So Ken related the story of his connection with the dead man. Jacques Verdier listened attentively, taking notes of points that interested him and occasionally interrupting with a question.

"So," he remarked when Ken had finished, "our Mr. Simpson was both a thief and a murderer. That's very interesting."

"Unfortunately, he appears to be that rare specimen, a criminal who contents himself with one successful crime—two in this instance, of course, but I have the impression that his wife's murder was the result of the theft of the gems."

"Yes," Verdier agreed, "Simpson appears successfully to have put his own criminal past behind him—it is difficult to tie it in with his own death. Nobody here now, and I think this includes his wife, seems to have had any connection with George Zillitch —except, of course, you yourself."

"Well, I didn't kill him. In fact, his death is undoubtedly costing me a handsome sum of money; enough to have allowed me to set up my own law practice and to keep me going the first hard years."

There was a silence as the commissaire thought about the story he had just heard.

"What you have just told me explains a good deal that puzzled me about the setup at the Auberge—the fact that Simpson had the hotel in his wife's name, that he had no bank account in France, that he led such a very retired life, apparently doing nothing but eating and sleeping."

"All through my search for him, I've run into the fact that the main thing anyone who had ever known remembered about him was that he was exceptionally interested in his food."

"But people don't get murdered because they're greedy. There has to be more of a reason than that."

"Such as?"

"An attractive woman might get tired of being made love to by a mountain of blubber."

"Madame Ariane?"

"Or the doctor. Or perhaps both. The gossip in the village is that they are lovers."

"If all lovers went about killing their legal mates, the problem of the population explosion would be as relevant as the question of how many angels can dance on the head of a pin."

"Still, sexual jealousy, or at least the desire to get rid of an unwanted spouse, has, through the centuries, been a common cause for murder. Now, to come back to the glass you purloined. Please tell me exactly what, to your knowledge, occurred the night of Simpson's death."

"I can do better than that," Ken replied. "I neglected to tell you that I took a movie of the whole thing up to the time I rushed back into the Auberge to steal the glass."

"A movie? What do you mean?"

"Ever since I got to l'Aber-Wrac'h I had been trying to see or get a picture of George Simpson. I changed my room until I finally got one from which I could see the Simpsons' living quarters—I could see and watch it, but I couldn't see *into* it. There were no rooms at the Auberge that would have permitted this. The private quarters consisted of a sitting room and a bedroom, but while I was there the light at night was mostly in the bedroom, rarely and only temporarily in the sitting room. I soon realized that my only chance of a good view into the room would be from the garden. So, on the night Simpson died, at about ten o'clock I went for a walk along the seafront, then turned up a road that ran behind the Auberge, got into the garden over the back gate, and found a spot from which I had a perfect, unimpeded view into the bedroom. Going back the way I came, I changed into something dark and waited until around two o'clock."

"The light in the bedroom was still on?"

"Yes. I'd noticed on previous nights that the room was never completely dark. Taking my camera, I let myself out of a back door of the Auberge and, to keep out of sight, made my way through the rhododendron bushes to the tool shed. But I must have made some noise because the center light in the room suddenly went on and Madame Simpson opened the window and stepped out on the terrace. For a moment she stood listening. 'Is that you, Léonie?' she finally called. When there was no answer, she walked to the edge of the terrace to see if she could see anyone, but it was completely dark and she finally went back in and shut the window. As soon as I was sure it was safe, I climbed up on the roof of the tool shed. I got my camera ready and from this vantage point I filmed what went on in the room. Madame Simpson went out of the door leading into the corridor and was gone for not more than about three minutes—we can time it from the film—while she was gone I focused on Simpson himself. He was awake. I saw him pick up what turned out to be a urinal from the floor and use it. Then Madame Simpson returned. She stood for a moment beside her husband's bed, then took the urinal into the bathroom. A few minutes later, she came out wearing a nightgown—she had been semidressed earlier—over which she slipped a dressing gown that hung over a chair. Presumably in answer to a knock, she opened the door and someone handed her a tray."

"Did you see who it was?"

"No. The door opens inward and Madame Simpson stood between it and my camera. She went over to the bed, helped her husband to sit up and pushed a pillow behind his back, then held the glass to his lips. He pushed her hand away and took the glass himself. She watched him for a moment, then turned back to the dresser on which she had set the tray, picked up a cup of tea, and sat down with it beside the bed. After about five minutes, Simpson handed her his glass and she put it and her cup back on the tray which she set on the floor outside the bedroom. I suddenly realized that glass would give me a perfect set of prints to compare with the Zillitch prints I had. I stopped the camera, made my way as noiselessly as possible back to the hotel, tiptoed down the corridor till I saw the tray on the floor, removed the glass, and hurried up to my room with it."

"So you have a photographed record of—"

"Everything that went on in that bedroom up to the time the tray was put outside the door."

"Fantastic! I wish we always had such means at our disposal."

"Big Brother?" Ken asked sardonically.

The commissaire laughed.

"I suppose you are right. The price would be too high. Better a few unsolved crimes. Where is this film?"

"It's here," and Ken opened his briefcase and handed over a metal container.

As soon as a projecter and screen had been prepared, the room was darkened and Ken's film was run off. It took eleven minutes. Twice more it was run off at this speed, then three times in slow motion. When it was over, and the curtains drawn back, Verdier turned to the American.

"Well, this exactly corroborates the account Madame Simpson gave me this morning. And if either Simpson himself or his wife slipped anything into that glass, it would have had to be done with all the skill of a prestidigitator." The policeman gave a sigh. "What with the motive and the opportunity, I was reasonably sure we were on the right track. Now I suppose we'll have to start all over again. Oh, well, that's a policeman's life for you. Meanwhile, I'd better have a heart-to-heart talk with this Mademoiselle Lafauve." He picked up the phone again.

"Get in touch with Anselm at the Auberge des Rochers—tell him to drop what he's doing and go through Mademoiselle Lafauve's effects *very* carefully. I'll be out there about six thirty."

CHAPTER XV

The name "Commissaire Verdier" had meant nothing to Letitia and, when he had asked for Madame Simpson, she had shown him the way to the linen room without giving the matter any thought. But news of this visit spread like wildfire among the staff, already aware of the gossip, and, when Letitia went to get her midmorning coffee, she found the kitchens buzzing with excitement. Knowing that the *commissaire de police* of Brest was with Madame Ariane, the staff, their heads together, discussed this new development in low voices. They fell silent when they saw the American girl and stared at her with curiosity.

"Well, what is your opinion?" the head waitress asked as she poured out coffee, added foaming hot milk, and handed the cup to Letitia.

"My opinion about what?" she asked.

"Do you think Madame Ariane killed Monsieur?"

"Why on earth would I think that?"

"The police do."

"The police?"

"Yes. Why else do you think Commissaire Verdier is with Madame Ariane now?"

Letitia's heart lurched; her own forebodings of the evening before, which she had succeeded in shaking off, came swarming back and, as she looked at the greedy, expectant expressions facing her, at these people wallowing in someone else's misery, she suddenly felt sick. She longed to say something that would quench the unhealthy enjoyment and wondered briefly what the atavistic reason was for this repulsive manifestation, down through the ages, to be so much more common in women than in men, particularly when one of their own sex was involved. But no words came. In the event, there was no need for her to speak; the group dispersed suddenly and silently. Mademoiselle Léonie was standing in the kitchen doorway, the basket on her arm heavy with fish.

Unable to drink much of her coffee, Letitia poured what was left down the drain and washed and dried her cup. When she got back to the reception desk, she noticed Ken McCabe's letters were no longer in his pigeonhole. He must have picked them up while she was in the kitchen, she reflected, and was annoyed that she had missed him. She longed for someone to tell her what was going on.

She was reading the paper when the Commissaire Verdier left the Auberge and she watched him get into the little police car and be driven away.

Things were exceptionally quiet; even the telephone rarely rang. Two guests stopped at the desk to check out of the hotel and waited while Letitia made out their bills; she cashed their traveler's checks, showed them on the map how to get to Mont St. Michel, and saw them drive away in a white Rolls-Royce, wishing she could drive away with them. Never had a morning seemed so long; she tried to read but the words meant nothing to her and she finally closed the book and sat staring at the familiar lobby. Suddenly she realized that the time had come to make a break in her life, that she was bored with the hotel business, bored with l'Aber-Wrac'h, bored with the Auberge, bored with Brittany, bored with France, and longed for the United States. Never in all her years had she been swept by such an intense feeling of homesickness. She even found herself yearning for the hamburgers, the fried clams, the spoon bread, the tender crisp chicken fried in a mixture of bacon fat and butter, and, even though she did not fancy desserts much, for the milk shakes that had to be eaten with a spoon, the sundaes with gobs of thick chocolate sauce over the scoops of vanilla ice cream, and the rich butter pecan cookies, for all of which her father's Strongholds were famous.

Getting out some paper, Letitia began a letter to him. Her pen raced across the sheets as she kept an eye on the clock. The one mail a day left l'Aber-Wrac'h at two thirty and she wanted no delay in getting the letter on its way.

"So, Dad, I'm going to give them a month's notice and come home," she finished. "They won't have any trouble replacing me—applications to work at the Auberge des Rochers flow in. It's been an interesting experience and, up to now, I've enjoyed it. But somehow the death of Mr. Simpson, even though it took place such a short time ago, has changed the whole atmosphere. It's funny, too, because he didn't have much to do with the place, yet there's something depressing, even unhealthy, about it now. This will probably pass and things will settle down but I've suddenly had it. Don't, however, expect that I'm going to go to work in a Stronghold. I've come to the conclusion that the hotel business isn't for me. Perhaps I'll try to get a job on a magazine, or go to work for some political party. Don't ask me which, they're both so awful. I wish someone would invent a new one—the Oligarch Party, for instance. Democracy is as ineffectual in running a country as in running a kitchen. The proverb 'Too many cooks spoil the broth' is true in either case.

"Give my best to Greta; I hope she and the kids are well."

Before Letitia went to have her usual early lunch, she hurried to the postbox to mail her letter. After lunch, she more or less resigned herself to the probability that once again she would have to work through the afternoon in view of the events earlier in the day. She was therefore surprised to see Madame Ariane appear punctually at two o'clock to take up her usual stint at the reception desk. Moreover, she was looking her usual attractive self again; the dark circles under her eyes had disappeared and the gray pallor of her face had given way to her more normal coloring, well set off by her mourning.

"You're looking much better," Letitia said, stepping down to make way for her.

"I had a bit of a headache earlier but I took some aspirin and I'm over it now," she said cheerfully.

"You're sure it's all right for me to go?"

"Yes, yes, of course. Run along and get some exercise. Please, if you don't mind, though, try to get back a few minutes before five. I have an appointment about then."

"Everything has been very quiet up to now and I'll be back here by four thirty," Letitia promised.

She had not long been gone when Ariane saw two little cars, their tops surmounted with the aerial and the golden ball which signified the police, drive into the courtyard. Five men in civilian clothes got out while one policeman, in uniform, remained with the cars. Ariane took a deep breath to try to still the wild beating of her heart; she was suddenly drenched in perspiration and she closed her eyes and willed herself not to faint. When she opened them again, one of the men was standing before her holding out a paper. She took it and unfolded it but she was unable to make sense of the words.

"What am I supposed to do?" she asked as soon as she was able to speak and her voice sounded high and tremulous in her own ears.

"It's a search warrant. I'd like the keys to your effects."

"My keys? I don't think anything is locked except, perhaps, my husband's desk. I can't remember. If it is locked, you'll find the key ring in my bag in my room. The key to the desk has a bit of red string tied to it."

"Where is your room?"

"Go through that door and it's the first on your left," Ariane replied, pointing to the end of the lobby.

"And where is Mademoiselle Lafauve's room?"

"Mademoiselle Lafauve? She shares my room."

"Are her things unlocked, too?"

"What's in the bedroom is, I think. I don't know about her office."

"Where is that?"

"Go through the dining room into the kitchen and ask someone there."

When the men had dispersed, Ariane closed her eyes and prayed, prayed that she would wake up and find that George's death and everything that had happened since had all been a nightmare. But, to her regret, she appeared to be quite awake.

The fact that the police were going through her papers did not particularly worry her. Her baptism and marriage certificates, an identity card, a batch of social security papers, the deed to the Auberge, and a few letters she treasured from hotel guests writing to tell her how much they had enjoyed their stay at the inn was about all she had in the way of documents. But the thought that someone was going through her personal effects made her feel unclean.

The afternoon dragged on. She was standing at the door looking at the police cars when Ken McCabe came up the steps.

"Visitors," she commented, pointing to the cars. "Very unwelcome visitors."

Ken looked at the two little cars.

"I expect soon even more unwelcome visitors will descend on you . . . the gentlemen of the press. If this had been Paris, you would have had them by this time."

"Yes, and I suppose after our names have been splashed over front pages all over the country, all our years of work here will have gone down the drain. It doesn't take very long to kill the reputation of a hotel. When will you be leaving?"

"Are you throwing me out?"

"I can't understand why anyone who can get away would want to stay here—now."

"Perhaps I'm in no better position to be able to get away right now than you are. We're in this together."

"We are?"

"We are," Ken replied. "And I think it's time you and I exchanged a few confidences. Is there anywhere we can go to talk? I have something to tell you."

"We can sit down here. I should be near the telephone until Letitia gets back. But I'm not sure I want to hear anything you can have to tell me . . . it sounds ominous."

"I think it's important for you to know about this, however."

"Oh, all right." And Ariane led the way to the nearest sofa. "What is it?" she asked when they had sat down.

"What I have to tell you may be something of a shock to you," Ken began.

"I've had so many shocks. One more or less won't make any difference. I have my second wind, now," Ariane replied, with an ironic smile.

"First, I must tell you why I came here."

"I suspected you were here for some purpose. It occurred to me that you were here because of one of the guests, but they have all left and you have stayed on. So I began to think that perhaps you were here because of Letitia."

"Because of Letitia?"

"I thought perhaps you were in love with her. She's an attractive child."

"She is and I think I am, as a matter of fact. But that is neither here nor there. I came here because of your husband."

"Go on."

So Ken once more told his story without, however, mentioning his own activities on the night of George Simpson's death. Ariane, her face stony, listened in silence, her hands tightly clasped on her lap.

"And I guess that's about it," Ken finally said.

"So, if what you tell me is true," Ariane said, looking up, "my husband was a thief and a murderer."

"I'm terribly sorry to add to your troubles," Ken replied.

"I'm too muddled right now to be able to think clearly," Ariane finally said. "But I'm not sure that you have added to them. In fact, in a queer way, I feel free. Free of the burden of gratitude, of responsibility. I can drop the whole thing. What I should like to do is walk out of here now, just as I stand, and never come back."

"You were not in love with your husband?"

"No. But I was grateful to him and now you tell me I no longer need be grateful. The funny thing is that the police think I killed George. I, who did everything I could to keep him alive. Of course, if George did what you say he did, I can't think why the police care what happened to him."

"You know they cannot take that point of view."

"I suppose they can't, though it seems to me his death saves them a lot of trouble and expense. Well, I suppose the only thing

to do now is to wait for whatever is going to happen next."
Ariane's eye was caught by the diamond ring on her hand. Taking it off, she held it out to Ken. "Here is a first installment for you
to return to your German friends."

"Don't be silly."

"Silly? Do you think I want it?"

"You don't know that my story is true, yet."

"I think it probably is. It makes sense and explains a lot that
was never clear. Here, take the ring."

"All that is for the future. Don't worry about it now."

"I may not have any future. Anyway, don't you realize the
sight of the beastly thing makes me sick? A stolen ring he gave
to the wife he murdered?"

"Lock it in a drawer or something."

"If you don't take it I'll throw it across the room . . . Please;
rid me at least of one of my burdens."

"All right. But only temporarily. This will all be straightened
out later."

Letitia walked through the lobby as he pocketed the diamond.

When she left the reception desk earlier, Letitia had run up to
her room to change her shoes, then made her way to her usual
hideaway on the beach. Since his trip to Paris the day George
Simpson died it had become routine for Ken McCabe to join her
during her free afternoon hours; on one or two occasions when
he had not been able to do so, he had told her beforehand. Anticipating this meeting and eager to talk to him, she had not
bothered to bring with her her usual books and writing materials. Today, however, she waited for him in vain. Several
times she started to leave, but the possibility that he might still
show up kept her from doing so. As the minutes dragged by,
feeling more and more aggrieved, she killed time by trying to
figure out what possible connection could exist between the
former narcotics agent and the Simpsons, because of whom, by
his own admission, he was staying at l'Aber-Wrac'h. But this
got her nowhere and when she returned to the Auberge a few
minutes before four thirty, she was tired and bored and very,
very cross.

She was alarmed to see, in the courtyard, two little police cars in one of which was seated the same policeman she and Ken had passed the day before, parked in front of the pharmacy. The other occupants of the car were presumably inside the Auberge and, with a sinking heart, Letitia hurried on in not knowing what to expect. Certainly it was not Ken McCabe and Madame Ariane seated on a sofa near the reception desk, so deep in their conversation neither seemed to see her. Passing them without a word, she went to her room to freshen up for her afternoon tour of duty. When she returned, Ken had left and Madame Ariane was standing at the front door alone, looking out. Just then a car drove up and a few moments later Dr. Le-Blanc ran up the steps. Madame Ariane opened the door to him. When he came in Letitia hardly recognized him. Gone were the espadrilles, the heavy blue sweater and the bluejeans. Instead, the doctor's black shoes gleamed, the gray flannel trousers he wore were neatly creased, a navy blue blazer perfectly fitted his broad shoulders, he was freshly shaven, and his hair had been cut and well brushed.

"What on earth caused *that* metamorphosis?" Letitia asked herself as she watched the two of them walk toward the little sitting room often used by the hotel guests as a card room.

"I hope you admire my elegance," the doctor said to Ariane as they sat down in armchairs by the window.

"I do indeed! What brought this about?"

"Annick insisted that I should dress properly if I was going courting."

"Oh, Yves, don't! This isn't the time. God knows what's going to happen next." And Ariane repeated what Ken McCabe had told her earlier in the afternoon. The doctor listened attentively. Where they were sitting they could talk without being overheard, though anyone crossing the lobby could see them. While they were there it seemed to Letitia, seated at her desk, that a remarkable number of the staff, most of whom were rarely seen in the front rooms of the Auberge, suddenly seemed to have urgent business there. Letitia was besieged with requests to buy stamps or to make telephone calls, and the lobby's ashtrays had never been so frequently wiped off.

Mademoiselle Léonie came by just after the two had stood up before separating; the doctor, holding both Ariane's hands in his own, kissed first one and then the other.

CHAPTER XVI

Commissaire Verdier was about to leave his office for l'Aber-Wrac'h when two of the men he had sent to the Auberge returned. He was surprised to see them so soon.

"What happened?" he asked.

"I went through the Simpsons' and Mademoiselle Lafauve's papers, as you instructed. Those of Mr. Simpson were all together in a folder which I have brought. They were very few: passport, *carte de séjour*, driver's license. No letters, bills, checkbook, or bank statements."

"He must have a safe-deposit box somewhere."

"I thought of that, but the only thing I found are these figures written here," and he pointed them out as he handed the manila folder to the commissaire.

"What about Madame Simpson?"

"Nothing of any particular interest; the usual documents, tax returns, bank statements, receipted bills, and so on . . ."

"Any passport?"

"No. Just a *carte d'identité*. There were also some *bulletins de paye* with her social security papers. She apparently used to be a typist at Assurances COPFEC. She couldn't have been a very good one—she was paid less than a thousand francs a month."

"Any letters?"

"Nothing personal. She did have a scrapbook filled with letters from satisfied clients praising the Auberge."

"What about Mademoiselle Lafauve?"

"She had a lot of papers in her desk. Old family papers—birth, death, and marriage certificates of parents and grandparents, a deed for a house in the Nord, a few letters from her mother, now dead. Then financial papers, tax returns, and her banking transactions. She's done very well since she changed from nursing to running a restaurant. She has over a quarter of a million francs in different savings accounts alone."

"You mean she used to be a nurse?"

"She was a senior nurse at the Hôtel Dieu in Paris."

"Until when?"

"Until she went to England for a year and then came here."

"That's very interesting. Did you get her account of the night of Mr. Simpson's death?"

"No. She flatly refused to talk to me at all. To every question I put, she answered that she would talk only to you, not to 'underlings.' "

"What about medicines?"

"They had been thrown away, but we were lucky. The trash collectors only go by once a week during the off season, so we were able to sift through the piles and found several medicine containers, some of them empty, some still with pills in them. They are in this," and the detective placed a small cardboard box on the desk. "I checked them with the pharmacy and they match Dr. LeBlanc's prescriptions. No digitalis containers. But there was this, which I found under the paper that lined the drawer of the night table beside Madame Simpson's bed." Here the detective took a small sealed plastic package out of his briefcase and handed it to his superior. "Pills."

"Did you find out what they were?"

"Not yet. I thought it would be better to do that here."

"Beside *Madame* Simpson's bed?"

"I don't know why I said that. The night table is between the two twin beds."

"So there is digitalis on the premises. One would have thought whoever used it would have destroyed whatever was left. Have those pills checked as soon as possible . . . and, by the way, you might have them checked for fingerprints as well. I don't at all know whether pills will take prints but you can find out. Meanwhile, I'll get along to the Auberge to have a little talk with Mademoiselle Lafauve."

"Better you than me; there is something about that woman's eyes that frightens me."

It was nearly six thirty when Jacques Verdier drew up at the Auberge. Letitia was at the desk.

"Is Mademoiselle Lafauve in?" he asked.

Letitia glanced at the time.

"She's in but a silver wedding dinner party is being held here this evening so she is probably busy in the kitchen. Shall I go to see?"

"I'll find my way." The commissaire walked across the lobby and into the dining room and Letitia watched him push the door leading into the kitchen.

Here, though everyone was busy, there was no disorder; in fact, the atmosphere was not unlike that of an efficient operating theater. When the kitchens had been installed, George Simpson had insisted on air conditioning and antinoise equipment. In spite of the vast coal-burning ovens, the place was cool and the normal racket of pots and pans was muted; this had gone a long way toward simplifying the problem of staff recruitment.

The commissaire found Mademoiselle Léonie watching while Suzanne, the dessert assistant, pounded walnuts, brown sugar, and cinnamon together in a mortar. They each tasted the result.

"Couldn't I add a little butter to the mixture?" Suzanne suggested. "I think it seems a little dry."

"When you roll the paste in the hot crepe the butter will melt," Mademoiselle Léonie replied thoughtfully. "I don't suppose that will matter, though. Add very little, then make one crepe and try it." She suddenly noticed the commissaire standing in the door.

"This is a fine kitchen you have," he said.

"Yes, one of the best in France. Is there something I can do for you?"

"Could you give me a few minutes of your time?"

"I suppose I can," Léonie said, glancing at her watch. "We'll go to my office."

"You know, of course, that the death of Mr. Simpson has be-

come a matter for police investigation," the commissaire said
as they sat down.

"Yes."

"My inspector told me you refused to answer questions he put
to you."

"Yes."

"Why?"

Léonie shrugged.

"I have my reasons. And it's such a bore having to repeat
things to different people . . . it's simpler to talk to the man at
the top."

"You're a very old friend of Madame Simpson?"

"Yes. I have known her since she was eighteen."

"And you have devoted yourself to her and to this Auberge?"

"I have been very fond of Ariane for a long time and, while I
don't wish to appear immodest, I feel that without me the Auberge would never have been the success it is."

"Did you like Mr. Simpson?"

"Oh, it was hard to *like* him. He was a man without much
personality. We had a common interest in food and its prepara-
tion."

"What was your impression of Mr. Simpson's background?"

"I don't know that I had one," Léonie replied. "He was an
American. It is always difficult to know too much about people
of a nationality other than your own."

"He must have had a good deal of money to buy and equip
this place. Where did you think this money came from?"

"Mr. Simpson was always very secretive about himself . . .
particularly about money."

"How did Madame Simpson meet him?"

A look of malice came over Mademoiselle Léonie's face.

"Through a matrimonial agency," she replied.

"I see. So neither Madame Simpson nor you knew anything
about Mr. Simpson's background when they married."

"No. I pointed this out to Ariane and told her I thought she
should find out more about the man she was planning to marry,
but she paid no attention to me."

"Did it occur to you that Mr. Simpson's money might have come to him illegally?"

"You mean he stole it?"

"Would you be surprised if you found that were the case?"

Léonie reflected for a moment.

"Yes and no," she finally answered. "As you mentioned, George Simpson had a good deal of money. Fools can steal small amounts of money, but it requires a certain amount of intelligence to commit larceny on a grand scale. Mr. Simpson seemed to me to have very little intelligence, which is why it would surprise me to learn that was how he got his money; not because I feel he would ever have had any moral scruples."

"I see."

"Did he steal the money?"

"This is a matter we are investigating. About Mr. Simpson's illness, I understand he was ill quite frequently, particularly during the last few months."

"Yes."

"What was the cause of his illness?"

"Obviously he ate too much and took practically no exercise. In addition to that, his doctor was a fool—or worse."

"What makes you say that?"

"Perhaps you are not aware of the fact that I used to be a nurse. If there is one thing nurses know almost instinctively, it is how to gauge the ability of doctors."

"And you didn't think much of Dr. LeBlanc's abilities. Why?"

"Perhaps I have a natural prejudice against military doctors. They are undoubtedly very effective in dealing with wounds incurred in war or in military exercises. But they are not particularly competent in other medical fields and are inclined to treat their patients as though they were malingerers."

"What did you mean when you said 'or worse'?"

For a few moments Léonie made no answer.

"I don't expect I'm telling you anything you don't know. Dr. LeBlanc is a poor man. Madame Simpson is not. It might well have occurred to him that, with Mr. Simpson out of the way,

Ariane would make a most satisfactory wife for himself—both well off and attractive."

"Are you suggesting that Dr. LeBlanc killed his patient?"

"I can think of no other explanation."

"Dr. LeBlanc says he prescribed no digitalis."

Léonie smiled ironically.

"He could have given Ariane the digitalis. It's easy enough for a doctor to procure."

"Madame Simpson says not."

"Ariane is very gullible. Anyway, the poor fool thinks he's in love with her."

"And you don't?"

"I think he's chiefly in love with the Auberge."

"Would you give me your account of what happened the night of Mr. Simpson's death?"

"I went to bed, as usual, about eleven thirty, first stopping by Ariane's room to see how her husband was and to ask if she didn't want me to stay with him for a while so that she could get some sleep. She had been up with him day and night for some time and was tired out. But she said Mr. Simpson was better and that she would rest later. So I went on up to bed."

"You didn't go downstairs again at all?"

"No."

"So it was not you who prepared Mr. Simpson's orangeade?"

"Heavens, no. I suppose it was Ariane."

The clear picture of the movie Ken McCabe had taken presented itself to the policeman. Someone had certainly come to the door and passed over to Ariane the tray, but all that could be seen was a pair of hands. Whose pair of hands?

"Your own explanation is that Mr. Simpson's death is due to Dr. LeBlanc."

"It's possible that Dr. LeBlanc made a mistake and inadvertently gave Ariane the wrong pills, which she put in her husband's drink. If she did put pills into George's drink, she would have had to do it secretly, because he refused to take medicines unless he was feeling very ill indeed."

But the movie had shown clearly that Ariane had put nothing

in the orangeade, either secretly or otherwise. The policeman decided on a frontal attack.

"Madame Simpson has stated that it was you who prepared the orangeade and also a cup of tea for her, and brought them on a tray to her room."

"Ariane said *that!*" Léonie exclaimed.

"Yes."

Léonie's eyes narrowed and she shook her head slowly.

"Poor, poor Ariane! It's even worse than I thought. I suppose he told her to say that . . . to lay the blame on me. He realized that I knew too much, that I knew that—"

"Yes?"

"It was Dr. LeBlanc who made the orangeade."

"Here? At three o'clock in the morning?" the policeman asked incredulously.

"He was frequently here all night. He and Ariane have been lovers for some time now. She and her husband formerly had an apartment upstairs near me. But she insisted on moving down to the ground floor . . . it is very simple to get into these rooms that give onto the garden without being seen. I know he has been here quite frequently during the weeks before George died. I saw him myself."

"You mean he came into her room with her husband in it?"

"Of course not. There are other rooms farther along this passage. At this time of the year we are rarely full."

"In other words, you think Madame Simpson and Dr. LeBlanc together poisoned Mr. Simpson."

"Never, never, never!" Léonie exclaimed. "Ariane is weak but she would never hurt a fly! It was all Dr. LeBlanc. If she actually put the digitalis in the drink she certainly didn't know what she was doing."

"But you say she lied to me when she told me it was you who brought the orangeade."

"If she told you that, yes, she lied to you. But *he* told her to tell the lie. And lying is not . . . murder."

Léonie stood up as she looked at the time.

"I must go. We are having a dinner party here tonight and there are still a few things I must check on."

Jacques Verdier closed his notebook and followed her out of the office.

*   *   *

The commissaire left the Auberge and sat in his car a few minutes before starting the engine. Then he drove straight home.

"Hard day?" his wife asked as he came in.

"Odd, rather than hard. If you add butter to the walnut, cinnamon, and sugar paste you use to stuff crepes, the butter is likely to melt."

"What?"

"It's a cooking tidbit I picked up at the Auberge des Rochers. I thought you'd be interested."

"We really must go there one day for dinner. I can't imagine why we never did. So many people have told me how marvelous it is."

"I'm afraid it's too late now," Jacques Verdier sighed.

He walked to the telephone and called his office.

"What prints besides George Simpson's were there on the glass that contained the orangeade?" he asked. "Just his and Mrs. Simpson's? No others at all? Thanks." He put down the receiver. That was not much help . . . or was it?

"If you have prepared an orangeade, aren't you bound to have touched the glass?" he asked his wife as they sat down to dinner.

"I should think so," she replied.

"So that if there are no fingerprints, wouldn't that mean that whoever prepared the drink either made a point of not leaving any—or wiped them off? And surely that would only be done if the person was very anxious indeed *not* to leave fingerprints— because he or she introduced something into the orangeade. If you were simply making ordinary orangeade, you wouldn't bother to wipe off fingerprints."

Madame Verdier considered this.

"I'm not sure what you're talking about but suppose you'd poured too much water into your orange juice so that it ran over, you might wipe off the glass and thus wipe off any fingerprints."

"But even then, wouldn't you be likely to touch the glass again as you set it down and so leave more fingerprints?"

"I suppose."

"I'm afraid I'm going to have to go out again after dinner," the policeman said with a sigh.

CHAPTER XVII

The French, from company president to assembly-line worker, adore vacations and usually succeed in wangling several three- or four-day weekends a year in addition to the month to which they are entitled by law. One of these long weekends was looming up and, the weather having unexpectedly turned fine, the exodus from city living to rusticity got under way and Letitia suddenly found herself very busy during her evening tour of duty. The telephone rang constantly as reservations for rooms and/or meals were made; a party of ten from a British yacht, which had sailed into the little port earlier in the afternoon, dined in the hotel and were enjoying a bibulous and somewhat noisy evening in the lobby of the Auberge. Ken McCabe approached the reception desk on several occasions, but Letitia coolly told him she had no time to talk to him. He retreated to a chair with a magazine, waiting for ten o'clock, when the night porter would come on. But at nine thirty Ken saw the commissaire at the front door beckoning to him; he followed the policeman outside.

"There are a couple of things I want to ask you and I don't want to come in right now," he said as they walked down the gravel path toward the gate. "I talked to the examining magistrate earlier this evening," he went on. "We have decided to issue a summons to the doctor, to Madame Simpson, to Mademoiselle Lafauve and to you to appear in my office tomorrow morning."

"I'll appear," Ken said. "And, by the way, I've told Madame Simpson about my connection with this mess."

"I'm not sure I am pleased that you did this without consulting me," Verdier said, with a frown.

"I did what I judged would be best for my client, Prince Altberg-Emringen, and, of course, what would be best for me."

"You told her the whole thing?"

"The whole thing, including an account of the presumed murder of Mrs. Zillitch."

"What did she say?"

"Her reaction was somewhat surprising. When she had grasped all the implications of the story I told her, she said she was relieved . . . that a burden had been lifted off her shoulders and she could now begin leading her own life. She also gave me this," and Ken drew the marquise diamond ring out of his pocket. "She said it was the first installment—that the Altberg-Emringen family would have returned to them everything that it was in her power to return."

"How very nice for your client!" Jacques Verdier commented, leaning on the stone wall as he looked at the blackness of the seascape.

"And for me," Ken reminded him as he lit a cigarette.

"And for you. I might even consider the possibility that the hands carrying the tray with the orangeade were yours. As you remember, all that could be seen in the movie you took was a pair of hands. This would make the fact that you so quickly obtained the glass with the fingerprints much easier to understand. Like me, the examining magistrate, Judge Fouillis, finds that coincidence quite remarkable."

"It is, of course, but then so are most coincidences. Let me give you an example. One day, walking past the bookstalls along the Seine, my eye was caught by a dog-eared, backless book that reminded me of the geometry book I had had at school. I stopped and looked at it and, by gosh, it *was* the geometry book I had had at school. My name and the date were scribbled in the front as well as the name of the boy who had had it before I did. How it got from Bismarck, North Dakota, to a bookstall in Paris I'll never know. However. It seems to me there are a considerable number of weak points in your argument trying to implicate me."

"I'm not trying to implicate you. I'm merely thinking out loud."

"Well, in your thinking, you should bear in mind two things.

One is that, far from having been on any terms of intimacy with Madame Simpson I had, in fact, really only glimpsed her from time to time. I certainly was not wandering around the Auberge at 3 A.M. getting orangeade for her husband."

"By your own admission, you were certainly wandering around the Auberge at 3 A.M."

"True. But don't forget that I was on top of the tool shed with my camera when the orangeade was handed in to Madame Simpson."

"I shall have to investigate since I know very little about cameras, but I suppose it is possible to set one to start filming at a certain time and then get in the picture yourself. After all, they send cameras up to invade the privacy of Venus and Mars and so forth with no photographers along."

"It may well be possible but I myself am not a professional and am not competent to do this, although this would be hard for me to prove. Also, I suppose you could always argue that I had someone along to work the camera while I was busy with my murder projects. But that brings up my second point. I had no reason to want George Zillitch or George Simpson, whichever you prefer, dead. Quite the contrary. All I wanted was to get him identified. Once I had proof that Major Zillitch and George Simpson were the same man, my job was done. The rest was up to lawyers. Why should I involve myself in the murder of a man I did not know, particularly when it suited me better for him to be alive?"

"Madame Simpson might have promised to make restitution without the necessity of resorting to lawyers. As, in fact, she has done."

"Oh, go boil your head," Ken exclaimed impatiently. "In the first place, you know damn well that lawyers have managed to get things fixed so that you can't even die without contributing to their well-being, let alone get involved with any kind of property. Anyway, you and your investigating magistrate can do as you like and believe what you want to believe, but if you intend to continue barking up that tree, you'll lose any quarry you might get altogether. Because your quarry is not up there."

"I'm inclined to agree with you," the policeman replied equably. "As I said, I was merely thinking out loud. One thing I'd like to ask you: do you have any personal impression of whether the tray was handed in the door by a man or a woman? At the time that it happened, did you say to yourself 'that's a woman' or 'that's a man'?"

"All I saw, I saw through the lens of the camera . . . which was a pair of hands."

"You had no instinctive feeling that they were a woman's hands? Or a man's hands?"

Ken thought for a moment.

"This is no sort of testimony and you must not let it influence you. I believe my impression was that the hands belonged to a woman, but that is chiefly because most of the staff at the Auberge are women. There are a few men on the place—I understand that the chef under Mademoiselle Lafauve is a man, though I have never seen him. And there is a combination porter and handyman. I've also seen a couple of men raking the gravel in the courtyard and working in the garden. But the staff is predominantly female. Which is probably the reason my instinctive thought was that the person handling the tray was a female. You must remember that I was chiefly focusing on the face of the man in the bed; I was not paying too much attention to what else went on in the room."

"Show me exactly the spot from which you took the pictures."

So Ken took the commissaire around to the back garden and pointed out the box from which he had climbed up to the roof of the tool shed. The commissaire pulled himself up and looked at the back rooms of the Auberge.

"There's nothing to see now," he said as he jumped down. "The curtains are closed. I wonder why they were open the night Simpson died."

"I can tell you that. You know the definition of a Frenchman as being a gentleman with a decoration, who invariably asks for more bread, who knows no geography, and who is afraid of drafts. Well, the first day I was here I heard one guest tell another that, while it was too bad Mr. Simpson was ill, at least as long as he was in bed he would not be coming around opening windows and doors all the time, creating drafts. Apparently Simpson liked plenty of fresh air regardless of the weather. Those long french windows which open inward catch and tear the curtains if these are closed and the window is open."

"I see. Well, I'll leave you now. I have another call I want to make tonight."

When Ken got back to the lobby, Letitia was no longer at the reception desk.

"Did Mademoiselle Strong go up to her room?" he asked the porter.

"I don't think so, monsieur. She said she had a headache and wanted a breath of air before going to bed."

Ken walked out to the gate again and looked up and down the road along the sea wall but could not see Letitia, so he returned to the hotel.

* * *

As they frequently did when they were alone, Ariane and Léonie had their dinner served in Léonie's little office near the kitchen. Even though the meal was a light one, both women, each busy with her own thoughts, ate little of it.

"Don't bother to come back," Léonie said to the waitress who had brought their coffee. "I'll wash the cups and put them away when we're through. Ariane," she went on when the woman had gone, "just what was the meaning of the scene of this afternoon in the card room?"

"Scene?"

"Yes. You know perfectly well what I'm talking about."

"Perfectly well," Ariane agreed. "But I'd hardly call it a scene. You might as well know, Léonie, that Dr. LeBlanc asked me to marry him and I have said I would."

Léonie's face went white.

"You . . . filthy . . . trollop!" she finally brought out from between clenched teeth. "What kind of a monster are you . . . your husband hardly buried and you talk about marrying the man who is responsible for his death!"

"Oh, rot, Léonie. You, of all people, know better than that."

"You vain fool! Don't you know the man wants your money?"

"That's too bad, then," Ariane shrugged. "Because I don't have any."

"You don't have any! Are you out of your mind?"

"Not at all. It's just that I've grown up, Léonie. It took me a long time but it has finally happened. Funnily enough, I grew up in one day. It's been a very tiring day but, on the whole, not an unhappy one." And Ariane, as succinctly as possible, repeated the story Ken McCabe had told her. "So," she ended, "what George gave me wasn't his to give. I shall return it to its owners. Don't worry, though, Léonie. This inn is really your creation. Anyone who takes it over will naturally want *you* to stay. You're well launched on the career you've always wanted and you should be happy."

"And you?"

"Don't worry about me. I never had your drive and ambition. All I ever wanted was a home and someone to love. You can't begin to imagine how lonely an orphan who knows nothing about her antecedents can be. I tried to love George, who may have been a criminal but who was good to me. So now I love someone else. It would be difficult to live here, with all the gossip, so Yves and I will probably go away—forever. I'm sorry about it because Yves loves it here, but it seems the best thing to do."

Léonie laughed shortly. Two red spots had appeared on her cheeks and her neck was mottled.

"You and your precious Yves may be going away forever, but not together," she said and her mouth spat the words out. "The police will see to that. They're not fools."

Ariane looked at her old friend impatiently.

"Oh, stop dramatizing," she said.

"You seem to forget that your husband was murdered," Léonie said from between clenched teeth.

Ariane shrugged.

"Perhaps. Or perhaps it was some sort of accident. Does it matter any more? Had he lived, he would have gone to prison—

and prison fare, for George, would have been a fate worse than
death. Things are just going to have to work themselves out as
best they can."

* * *

When Letitia left the hotel, she had seen Ken talking to the
commissaire, so she turned to the right to avoid passing the two
men. It was a clear, moonlit night and since she loved to look
at the graceful sailing boats and yachts in the harbor, she made
her way toward the little jetty. As she drew near the benches,
she recognized Ariane seated on one of them. During the time
she had been at l'Aber-Wrac'h Letitia had, on a few occasions,
seen the hotel owner taking a sedate stroll with her husband,
but she had never seen her out alone. Now, when Madame Ariane recognized the girl, she waved.

"Come and sit down," she called. "It's a beautiful evening. I
can't bear to go back. Aren't the yachts pretty?"

Letitia sat down on the bench beside her employer and it occurred to her that this would be an appropriate moment to tell
her that she intended to leave in a month.

"I hope it won't inconvenience you," she ended up.

The hotel owner hardly seemed to be listening.

"Will this be all right with you?" Letitia insisted.

"What? Oh, yes," Madame Ariane said vaguely. "You must
go when you like. As a matter of fact, I'm going away, too."

"I expect a change and a rest would do you good. You've had
a bad time lately. Where are you going?"

"I don't know, yet. All this trouble about my—about Mr. Simpson's death makes things difficult. But I'm not going away just
for a rest; I'm going away definitely."

"You mean you're leaving the Auberge?" Letitia asked, surprised. "What will happen to it?"

"It's really been Mademoiselle Léonie who runs it. She will
probably just go on. To tell the truth, I don't at all care what
happens to it." Suddenly she shivered. "I'm getting cold; I'd better go back," she added, standing up.

They were both silent as they returned to the Auberge. Just before they reached it, Ariane stopped.

"Would you mind doing something for me?" she asked Letitia. "Mademoiselle Léonie and I had an argument earlier this evening. I'm still a little upset and would rather be alone. I'll take one of the empty rooms but I need my things. What I wish you would do is to pick up my nightgown, slippers, and toothbrush from our room. I would rather not see Mademoiselle Léonie again tonight."

"Of course I will," Letitia agreed. "There is no one in thirty-five. Why don't you take that and I'll bring your things up to you there."

They entered the Auberge by a side door and, while Madame Ariane picked up the key of 35, Letitia crossed a corner of the lobby and walked down the passage toward the suite occupied by the two managers of the Auberge. There was no answer to her knock at the door, so she opened it and tried to turn on the light.

"Damn, the bulb's gone," she said to herself as the click of the switch failed to produce light.

There was a transome over the door and Letitia stood still for a moment to allow her eyes to adjust to the semidark, then groped her way toward what she took to be the bathroom door. There was a sound of a door being locked behind her; she turned and cried out, but something was drawn across her throat and was choking her. She tried to struggle with her unseen assailant but a tighter squeeze blocked out consciousness.

* * *

Ken McCabe, from the lobby, caught a glimpse of Letitia's red sweater as she turned into the passage leading to the rooms that gave on the gardens. He hurried after her and was just in time to see her go into Madame Ariane's bedroom. Suddenly he heard what sounded like a strangled cry. He went to the door and as he stood outside listening, he thought he detected the muffled sounds of a struggle. He knocked peremptorily and tried the handle, but the door was locked.

"Letitia!" he called urgently. "Are you all right?" A dull thud was the only answer. Putting his shoulder to the panel, he tried to break in but the door was a solid one and the passage was too narrow to allow him to attack the panel at a run.

"Open the door, quickly!" Ken called, kicking at it with all his strength. He was about to go for help when two members of the yachting party, searching for the toilet, appeared at the end of the passage.

"Give me a hand," Ken called, panting. "I've got to get in there!"

"What the bloody hell's up?"

"Life and death. We'll all heave together. One, two, three, go!"

At the third shove, the door splintered open and Ken fell into the room. A blow on his head nearly knocked him out but he managed to turn and, in the light from the corridor, he saw Léonie Lafauve, her upraised arm clutching what appeared to be the base of a lamp, prepared to strike again. Ken tried to jerk her legs out from under her but she fought him off and, breaking away, made a dash for the next room. Ken, starting to follow, stumbled on something soft. He found a light switch that worked: Letitia, purple in the face, the cord still tight around her neck, was lying on the floor. Ken, with a gasp, cut the cord, lifted the light form on to the bed and began to breathe into the girl's mouth.

The noise had brought the rest of the yachting party as well as the night porter to the room.

"Quick, call the doctor and the police," a voice said. "Where did the other woman go?"

Ken, without interrupting his efforts to restore Letitia's breath, pointed toward the next room. But Léonie had had time to lock that door, too. While the porter, with shaking fingers, telephoned Dr. LeBlanc, two of the Englishmen tried to force it open while the third ran out on the terrace. As he was smashing the french window a shot was heard, and when they finally got in, Léonie was lying on the bathroom floor, dead.

CHAPTER XVIII

After leaving Ken McCabe at the Auberge, the commissaire Verdier climbed the steep hill leading up to Dr. LeBlanc's cottage. It was the doctor himself who opened the door.

"I thought there was some law in France which prevented the police from arresting a man in his own home between sunset and sunrise," the doctor said with a frown, glancing at his watch. "Ten P.M. seems well after sunset."

"It is and you are quite right," the policeman replied. "I could arrest you on the street or in some public place, assuming I had a warrant, but not in your own home. However, I haven't come to make any arrests, an occupation which, if it is at all possible, I leave to others. But I should like to talk to you for a few minutes and I think you will be interested in what I have to say. May I come in?"

Dr. LeBlanc shrugged and led the way to his study.

"I'm just about to have a cup of coffee. Will you join me?"

"With pleasure."

The doctor went to the head of the stairs.

"Annick!" he called.

"Monsieur?"

"Two cups when you bring the coffee, and also a bottle of the Calvados Guy Morin gave me for Christmas. One of my patients distills a superlative cider brandy; it's as smooth as silk for all its punch," he added, coming back into the room and waving the policeman into one of the two leather armchairs before the fireplace.

"How is your investigation going?" he went on.

"I believe I have come to the end of it."

The doctor sat up in his chair abruptly.

"What!" he exclaimed. "You know who killed George Simpson?"

"There is still a good deal of work to be done, but the examining magistrate agrees with me that the time has come to interrogate several of the witnesses, including you. Here is your summons to appear at ten tomorrow morning." And Verdier handed the doctor an envelope, which the latter glanced at.

"That will throw my schedule out," he grumbled. "And to what do I owe the honor of your present visit?" he added as he pocketed the summons.

"There are one or two questions I should like to put to you unofficially."

"I'll be glad to answer if I can."

"Looking back on the history of Mr. Simpson's illness, have you thought at all about what possibly could have caused the gastric attacks he had earlier, the attacks from which he recovered?"

"I have, of course. In fact, I went through his medical history quite thoroughly after I learned of the autopsy."

"Could these attacks have been induced?"

"Yes, of course."

"Do you have any suggestions as to how, in fact, they were brought on?"

Dr. LeBlanc took some time to light his pipe before he answered.

"There are various drugs which could be used to bring on attacks of stomach trouble. It's a coincidence that you should ask me that this evening, however. Just before you arrived Annick, my housekeeper, was telling me that she thinks she has an answer to your question . . . in fact, she is sure she has."

"Really? And what is her opinion?"

"I'll let you talk to her yourself. Before I call her, though, you should know that her great interest in life is in plants and their medicinal properties. Her mother and grandmother were both well known around the countryside as herbalists, and Annick has carried on the family tradition. She is also, of course, a superb gardener." He opened the door and went to the head of the stairs.

"Annick!" he called. "Come up here, please. We want to talk to you."

"I'm coming," she answered.

"This, as you know, is the commissaire Verdier," the doctor went on when she was in the room. "He wants to hear about Mademoiselle Léonie's garden."

"M. Yves, that was for your ears only," the old woman said reproachfully.

"I'll be discreet, Mademoiselle Annick," the policeman replied. "Please tell me about the garden. I'm very much interested."

"It was just that I was saying to M. Yves that, if anyone wanted to cause stomach upsets, Mademoiselle Léonie's garden has many plants that would do it. Plants can save lives and restore health, but they can also cause sickness and even kill."

"What plants were you thinking of, Mademoiselle Annick?"

"There are very many."

"Tell me about the ones that are in Mademoiselle Lafauve's garden."

"In the first place, there is the wisteria that she planted at the back gate . . . the seeds and pods can cause serious stomach ailments and yet the taste is quite pleasant. Then, in the flower garden, Mademoiselle Léonie has a lot of larkspur. The seeds of larkspur cause nervous excitement followed by depression and they can easily be mixed with salad. Daphne berries can be fatal; there is also a great deal of foxglove, which is used to stimulate the heart."

"Isn't foxglove the source of digitalis?" the commissaire asked Dr. LeBlanc.

"One of them. I suppose if enough were taken, the result might be a digestive upset accompanied by mental confusion, but it would require a good deal and I find it hard to believe that Simpson, who was particular about his food, could have been induced to swallow large quantities of the flower."

"It is easy to make a tea from the leaves," Annick pointed

out. "When my uncle had a sudden heart attack my mother saved his life with foxglove tea."

"What other plants in that garden are potentially dangerous?"

"Crocus, lily of the valley, and iris can all make you very sick, and these are all present at appropriate seasons. Then laurel, rhododendron, and azaleas can be fatal and so can jasmine berries. The difficulty would be to prepare them in a palatable way. But because I tell you this, I don't mean that I think Mademoiselle Léonie—"

Just then the telephone rang and Dr. LeBlanc went to answer it.

"Dr. LeBlanc speaking," he said. Suddenly he stiffened. "What!" he exclaimed. "Good God! Call two ambulances, quickly. I'll be right there." He turned to the commissaire. "That was the porter at the Auberge. There has been an attempt to murder the young American girl who works there. The porter is not sure whether she is dead or not. I'm going down the back path—it's quicker than driving."

And the two men hurried out into the night.

"Who is the second ambulance for?" the commissaire asked as they slithered down the steep path.

"Mademoiselle Léonie. She shot herself."

"Is she dead?"

"The porter seemed to think so."

"Well, as Talleyrand remarked when informed of the death of his wife, 'Ça simplifie les choses,'" the policeman said as they turned in to the Auberge.

CHAPTER XIX

In France, the underpaid provincial press is somewhat som-
nolent and dislikes having its routine disturbed. It dutifully
prints government-subsidized wire service material on national
and international affairs, reports speeches by local politicians,
sports news, the more lethal motorcar accidents, and crop
damage caused by storms. Cows, sheep, and even humans
struck by lightning are also considered newsworthy. Enormous
headlines are used as space fillers; the less there is of news the
blacker and larger the headlines.

The only mention of George Simpson's death was in the
obituary notices sent by the various mayors' offices to their local
paper. In Dinard, however, a vacationing American reporter
from one of the wire services, hotel-bound by bad weather,
picked up the local ten-day-old paper and, having nothing else,
read it from cover to cover. His eye caught the names "Simpson"
and "l'Aber-Wrac'h" and he remembered that he had once had a
fabulous meal at the Auberge des Rochers and had even done a
short human-interest piece about this excellent inn run by an
American. The rain showed no signs of letting up and, bored,
the reporter decided to drive to l'Aber-Wrac'h to find out what
was going to happen to the inn now that the owner was dead.
If there was any kind of a story there, he would be able to have
dinner and spend the night on expense-account money.

Engine trouble delayed him so that the first part of his pro-
gram had to be abandoned, and he ate an undistinguished meal
while repairs were made; he arrived at l'Aber-Wrac'h just in
time to see two ambulances drive away from the Auberge, sirens
screaming.

An hour later he was on the telephone to his office and the

next day an army of newsmen, led by a solid phalanx of Americans, descended on l'Aber-Wrac'h.

* * *

Letitia had only moments of consciousness during her first days in the hospital at Brest, but consciousness meant pain and she was glad to slip back into drug-induced nirvana. The resilience of youth and her normal good health asserted themselves, however, and one sunny morning she woke up to find that the pain had become mere discomfort and that her voice had come back.

"What on earth happened to me?" she asked the nurse when she came into the room.

"You're looking much better," the latter said. "How do you feel?"

"My neck is still a little stiff, but I seem to be all right otherwise. Did I have an accident—I can't seem to remember things. How long have I been here?"

"Five days. Do you think you will be able to swallow if I bring you up something to eat?"

"I think so. I know I'm horribly hungry. Haven't I eaten for five days?"

"We fed you intravenously."

"Ugh! No wonder I'm hungry."

"I'll bring you something at once." At the door the nurse met Dr. LeBlanc coming in. "I was just going to call you, Doctor. Mademoiselle seems very much better."

"Good! Ken McCabe will be delighted to hear the news. He has worn out the carpet in our waiting room, pacing the floor."

"What I want to know, Doctor, is what happened to me. I seem to have had a spell of amnesia."

"I'll leave all that for Ken to tell you. Now let's see how you are."

"I guess you'll live," he finally said, with a grin, when he had completed his examination. "For a while you certainly had us worried. Incidentally, you might like to know that you owe your life to Ken McCabe's quick thinking."

"But, Doctor, what *happened?* The last thing I remember was talking to Madame Ariane as we were walking back to the Auberge."

"A good deal happened after that, all very distressing. It's a long story and I haven't the time to tell it myself. I'll send Ken in to bring you up to date."

"Where is Ken?"

"About half an hour ago he was beating off the newspapermen who wanted to force their way in to talk to you. You're famous, young lady."

"Famous? Me? What on earth— I'm going to die of curiosity."

"You'll hear all about it in half an hour or so," the doctor promised, going toward the door. "First, you must try to take some nourishment, and I expect nurse will want to tidy you up a bit."

The nurse came in with a tray just then and, after exchanging a few words with her, he left the room.

Letitia had succeeded in swallowing about half a cup of strong beef broth, she had been bathed, her hair had been combed, the nurse had produced a pretty nightgown and matching bed jacket the provenance of which she said she had been instructed to keep secret, and she was lying in her freshly made bed, feeling reborn, when Ken came in carrying a pile of newspapers.

"Hi, there, beautiful," he said coming up to the bed. "Well, gosh, you *are* beautiful."

"It's just that I've had my face washed. Anyway, don't sound so surprised! And, Kenneth McCabe, if you don't tell me immediately what the hell this is all about, I'll . . . I'll . . . I can't think of anything bad enough to do to you."

"I'll tell you, but I thought you might like to have a gander at these," and he spread the pages of various newspapers across the bed. To Letitia's astonishment, these featured pictures of herself, of the Auberge, of Dr. LeBlanc, of Madame Ariane, of George Zillitch (alias Simpson), of Edna Mae Zillitch (née Jones), of Ken, of the Altberg-Emringen jewels and of the princely couple standing outside their schloss.

Letitia picked up one of the papers and began to read.

"For God's sake!" she finally breathed, her eyes wide with wonder. "Is all this fantastic story true?"

"In the main. There are some inaccuracies and some exaggerations, but on the whole it's an account of what happened."

"And Mademoiselle Léonie really did try to strangle me?"

"She nearly succeeded. But, of course, she thought you were Ariane."

Letitia turned back to the paper.

"So I was right. The reason you came to the Auberge was because you were looking for Mr. Simpson—I mean Zillitch."

"Yes, but, of course, I didn't realize that I was stumbling on a murder."

"Dr. LeBlanc told me—and it says it here, too"—and Letitia pointed to the paper—"that you saved my life." She looked up at Ken and tears rose to her eyes. "To say thank you just sounds silly. There are no words in the English language to cover what one feels in such a case."

Ken leaned over and kissed the girl's forehead.

"No thanks are due. If it hadn't been for my butting in, you wouldn't have been in any danger."

Letitia frowned.

"I'm not quite sure I follow that. Anyway, if you hadn't 'butted in,' as you call it, Mademoiselle Léonie would have gotten away with murder!"

"A good many people do, from time to time, particularly if they don't start making a habit of it. At least Mademoiselle Léonie's victim pretty much deserved what he got."

"She didn't know that, though," Letitia pointed out. "What has happened to the Auberge, by the way?"

"That's another story. First, I must tell you that I have talked to your father on the phone several times and he's arriving tomorrow."

"Dad's coming here? Good heavens! Because of me?"

"Well, partly. I reassured him about your health but he decided to come to Europe anyway. Is 'Greta' his wife?"

"Why?" Letitia asked cautiously.

"He said something about having a spot of trouble about Greta."

"Oh, dear, I had so hoped Greta would last."

"She is his wife, then."

"Yes. His fifth. Dad's addicted to matrimony," Letitia said despondently. "He's from Kansas and I guess it's the puritan ethic. I shocked him terribly when I suggested it would be cheaper if he didn't bother to go through a ceremony. It seems he can't operate effectually as a husband without, so to speak, his marriage certificate under his pillow. It's an awful bore, all this chopping and changing. And I'm so *tired* of being tactfully sympathetic to a string of stepmothers."

"Don't you like any of them?"

"Oh, yes. In fact, I've liked all of them but one. That's what makes it so frustrating. Still, it'll be nice to see Dad. He's a grand guy when he's not busy courting, which, if I know him, he probably will be. It's always 'off with the old and on with the new' with him and he's very susceptible, particularly to nice legs. If he isn't already involved, he'll probably meet someone on the plane on his way here. Greta was a Swissair stewardess."

"Does he never have any trouble getting women to marry him?"

"With all those Strongholds going for him? You must be kidding!"

"The Strongholds, by the way, are another reason he is coming. He told me, and you probably know all about it, that he is thinking seriously of starting a European chain and wants to investigate the situation first hand."

"Yes, we talked about it before I came to l'Aber-Wrac'h. Those poor Europeans! Toasted cheese sandwiches with one and one eighth ounce of cheese and plenty of ketchup within easy reach of everybody."

"It'll probably be Americans homesick for ketchup that will make up the bulk of his clientele. Right now, I think he's proposing to start the chain by making an offer for the Auberge."

"Oh, dear! Well, when he gets here I'll try to head him off that." Letitia picked up one of the papers on the bed which carried her picture on the front page. "This is awful!" she exclaimed. "How will I ever live it down? I'll have to change my name."

"What a coincidence! I was just going to suggest that," Ken replied.

"You were going to suggest that I change my name?"

"Yes. I was going to propose that you change it to McCabe. 'Letitia McCabe' would look nice on the dust jacket of a novel, don't you think?"

"Ken! Don't be a dope!"

"I like that! Here I am proposing matrimony and you tell me not to be a dope. Of course, I realize proposing matrimony isn't much done these days. Couples just flop down on the nearest bed. The trouble about that is that the bed you're now in looks so damn hard and hygienic and, moreover, I don't think the nurse would like it if I joined you there. Anyway, I'm the old-fashioned type. I even went so far as to ask your father's permission to propose to you. How's that for pure Jane Austen?"

"Ken, you nut!" Letitia laughed. "What on earth did Dad say?"

"Actually, all he said after I'd repeated myself the third time was that there must be something wrong with the connection. So I'm really proposing without your parent's permission, Miss Strong. But I would indeed be most honored if you would become my wife. And, if you want to know what our financial prospects are in life, they're not bad at all. Prince von Altberg-Emringen is doing nobly by me. My first venture in the field of private enterprise has been crowned with success."

"What are you going to do with your new wealth?"

"Subject to your veto, I plan to go home to North Dakota, set up a law practice, and, if I find an opportunity, perhaps go into politics. Someone once said that war was too serious a business to be left to generals. I think politics is too serious a business to be left to politicians."

"But if you go into politics, you'll *be* a politician."

"A new breed of one. May I offer you the prospect of a choice residence at 1600 Pennsylvania Avenue, Washington, D.C.?"

"Under no circumstances!" Letitia answered. "I don't want a

house thousands of people can tramp through every day and that has only a four- to eight-year lease. I want a place of my own. Anyway, where's my ring? I can't be engaged without a ring."

"Mercenary!" Ken said as he put his hand in his pocket. "You thought you had me there, didn't you? But I fooled you," he added, bringing out a jeweler's box.

"You conceited thing! You certainly are sure of yourself!"

"Not really. I just brought it along in the *hope* that I'd succeed in sweeping you off your feet. It belonged to my mother and I thought it might do until I could buy you another." And Ken slipped a ring on her finger, the setting of which consisted of a large black pearl, flanked by two white ones.

"It's beautiful," Letitia said as she surveyed her hand. Then she looked up at Ken. "It seems to me I remember that Mr. Darcy embraced Elizabeth when they got engaged, since we're being so Jane Austenish. Do I have to wait until *after* the ceremony before I get kissed?"

"Ralph and Rosemary, Hillary and Hugh," Ken said a few minutes later.

"*Regan* and Rosemary," Letitia corrected. "But let's not have twins. It'll be more fun to string 'em out."

CHAPTER XX

Dr. LeBlanc and Ariane were married quietly in l'Aber-Wrac'h and a month later Letitia and Ken had their wedding in the little chapel of the Schloss Altberg. Letitia wore the Worth gown and priceless lace veil of the prince's great-grandmother, and the prince himself served as Ken's best man.

The Auberge des Rochers escaped the fate of being the first of the "Stronghold Europe S.A." chain. It was saved by the party of Englishmen who had been dining there the night of Letitia's ordeal. The collapse of Ariane and the death of Mademoiselle Léonie left the inn rudderless and, gourmets to a man, they simply took over its management, bribing the chef, who showed signs of wanting to move to a less homicidal locality, to remain at his post, promising him there would be no more murders or attempted murders.

The flight of the real wealth of Britain, which will ultimately leave the country with a few nonprofitable socialized industries, is a phenomenon of the times and the well-heeled, in an endeavor to escape confiscatory taxation and strikes ruinous to profit, more and more seek investment opportunities on the Continent of Europe. Since the hotel and food industries in France, fragmented and casually run, offer excellent prospects for gain, it was precisely to look into the possibility of finding something in this field that the yachting party had come to France. The Auberge almost literally fell into their hands, to everyone's satisfaction, and its high standards were maintained.

The horrendous legal snarls involved in determining the ownership of the funds in George Simpson's bank account in Switzerland (the number of which Ariane had found on a manila folder) and of the Auberge des Rochers was a source of jubilation to the army of lawyers required to untangle them.

Ariane LeBlanc steadfastly refused to accept any portion of her late husband's ill-gotten gains, and the Prince von Altberg-Emringen just as steadfastly insisted that a portion of the proceeds of the sale of the Auberge was her due since it was in part her work which had helped make it a success.

This matter was finally settled to the prince's satisfaction when Ariane gave birth to a daughter. He set up a trust fund for the child which was to be terminated and the principal paid over to her at the time of her marriage or when she was twenty-five, whichever event came first.

POSTSCRIPT

Having, over the years, received quite a few requests for recipes of dishes I occasionally mentioned in various books, I decided, since this volume dwells a good deal on matters gastronomic, to give a few in this postscript in case any readers might be interested.

The recipes set forth below should be fairly foolproof. I have used them for years in all parts of the world and have had to adapt them to different types of ingredients and various means of cooking—kerosene stoves, braziers, chulas, coal and wood ranges (some of which refused to function if the wind was in the wrong direction), and, once in a long while, I got a chance to use a proper modern gas or electric range with automatic heat control.

Léonie Lafauve's dinner for Ariane and her fiancé is, I suppose, the logical starting point.

Insofar as the spinach is concerned, all I can add is that I use four pounds of spinach and remove the tough stems before cooking, without adding water. I have never tried using frozen spinach.

Nor is there much I can add with regard to the roast breast of veal since I have been fairly explicit as to how Léonie made it. The difficulty about making a good roast of this sort in the U.S. is that the veal is unlikely to be milk-fed and, unless you are on very good terms indeed with your butcher, it is not easy to procure a whole breast properly cut. Frequent basting and long slow cooking helps even an inferior piece of meat. When I prepare this myself, I do not bother about lining the pocket with smoked ham. I make an ordinary sage stuffing (day-old bread shredded, finely chopped onions, salt, sage, melted butter), replacing some of the melted butter with bacon fat, which I obtain from frying two ounces of slab bacon, cut into tiny cubes, till crisp. I also add this bacon, well drained, to the stuffing.

POTATO PIE

Line a pie pan with any good, short flaky pastry (I use rough puff pastry). Slice thin as many potatoes as you need to fill the pie; this depends on its size. I usually use a 10-inch pie plate. Drop the potato slices in rapidly boiling water and cook for about 3 minutes. Remove the slices at once and lay them on a towel to drain. Dry them thoroughly.

Line the pie with a layer of potatoes, add salt, pepper, and melted butter, put in another layer of potatoes, again add seasoning and butter, and repeat till the pie is full. Lay strips of pastry latticelike over the potatoes and put in hot oven till pastry begins to brown. Turn down heat to moderate (350°) and continue cooking. When pie is half cooked, pour as much thick cream as the potatoes will absorb through each of the openings of the lattice. Return to oven and finish cooking. This is very, very good.

GÂTEAU ISABELLE

Grind up 1½ cups of roasted almonds, skins removed. Melt 8 ounces of sweet baking chocolate with 2 tablespoons of milk or cream over hot water. Cream ¾ cup of soft butter with 1½ cups of very fine sugar (not icing sugar, however) until light. Beat in almonds and chocolate mixture till well mixed, then gradually beat in cream. Turn into an 8 x 4 x 2-inch loaf pan and refrigerate overnight.

A friend of mine once told me about the extraordinary appetizers she was served—the cigar-shaped pancakes filled with pâté—with which Léonie began her dinner. I regret to say that I have never tasted these myself nor have I ever tried to make them. Unless the egg and bread-crumb mixture acts as a sealer, I don't quite see what prevents the pancakes from unrolling when they are fried or, for that matter, why the pâté would not melt. Perhaps very hot deep fat is the answer. If anybody wants to try this I'd be happy to know the result.

That takes care of Léonie's dinner party.

Now for the teas at the Auberge des Rochers.

The three following recipes from my grandmother's cookbook, written in her fine Italian hand, were favorites for high tea when I was a child and, with a bowl of soup, they make a filling, nourishing, and inexpensive supper today. Whenever I prepare any one of the three, there is never a crumb left.

SINGIN' HENNIES (OR HINNIES)

½ pound plain flour (2 cups)
1 teaspoon baking powder
¼ teaspoon salt
2 ounces butter or fat (lard or other shortening)

1 ounce sugar
Handful of currants
Milk

Sieve flour, baking powder, and salt. Rub in butter till you get quite coarse crumblike pieces. Add sugar and currants and enough milk to make a dough you can handle. Flour your hands and make one 8-inch round (or two smaller ones) and place on a *hot* greased griddle (spelled "girdle" in my grandmother's cookbook) till brown (about 7 minutes). Then turn and cook on other side. Butter while hot and serve with or without honey. One 8-inch singin' hennie may be cut in four parts, but this does not by any means indicate that it is enough for four people. It depends entirely on how much they like singin' hennies. The name, incidentally, comes from the fact that they "sing" as they cook.

FAT RASCALS

2 cups flour
Pinch of salt
¼ pound butter
1 heaping tablespoon brown sugar

Currants
Milk
White sugar

Sieve flour and salt into warm bowl. Rub in butter, add brown sugar and currants. Stir together with enough milk to make a soft dough. With floured hands, put on floured pastry board and roll out ¼ inch thick. With a glass or biscuit cutter, cut into rounds. Dust *heavily* with white sugar. Lay on a baking sheet and bake 10–12 minutes in a hot oven (about 450°). Fat rascals are only good hot, but they can be made ahead and then reheated. They need neither butter nor honey; on the other hand, they do not spurn either or both.

SCOTCH PANCAKES

The following recipe of my grandmother's is quite different from most I have seen for Scotch pancakes, which seem to involve eggs. I much prefer the version given below, which is simplicity itself.

1 cup sour cream*	1 level teaspoon baking soda
A pinch of salt	Flour

Mix all ingredients, using enough flour to make a dough thick enough to roll out. (Actually, I divide the dough in three pieces and pat each one flat with my hands, thus eliminating the chore of cleaning off the rolling pin and the pastry board.) Each pancake will be quite large. Cook them one at a time in a perfectly dry well-seasoned cast-iron frying pan (or on a griddle) that is not too hot. Cook very slowly till brown and crisp on one side, turn with a spatula, and serve with butter and/or honey.

DEVONSHIRE (OR CORNISH) SPLITS

2 ounces yeast	1 ounce lard
1 teaspoon sugar	¼ pound butter
½ pint warm water	½ cup milk
1½ pounds flour	1 teaspoon salt

* Whipping cream or condensed milk soured by adding vinegar or lemon juice is more satisfactory than commercial sour cream, which has less fat content.

Put the yeast in a bowl with sugar, add warm water and then a tablespoon of the flour. Let this rise in a warm place while you put lard, butter, milk, and salt in a saucepan and heat. Put the rest of the flour in a mixing bowl, make a well in the middle, and pour in the milk, etc., and the yeast mixture. Mix into a soft dough and put to rise. When risen, knead, roll out and cut into small rounds. Place these on a baking tin and let rise again. Bake in a moderate oven about 40 minutes. When they are cooked, brush over lightly with melted butter or oil and place them on a warm blanket, covering lightly with same. This is to prevent their getting crisp.

To serve, split about three quarters of the way. Put some strawberry jam (or, as we frequently did, crushed sugared strawberries) at the attached end and add a thick gob of Cornish (or Devonshire) cream.

CLOTTED CREAM (OR CORNISH OR DEVONSHIRE CREAM)

It's hardly worth my while telling anybody how to make Cornish cream since few people today are able either to lay their hands on "raw" (i.e., straight from the cow) milk, nor do they have an old-fashioned range on which you can keep things warm without actually cooking them. On the off chance that somebody *is* able to combine these two essentials, I give the following recipe.

Fill a shallow pan with evening's milk and leave till morning. Then place at the back of the stove. Leave till a thick crust forms (about 1 hour). Do *not* allow it to boil. Put it in a cool place and leave it a day to thicken. Roll the crust off. The liquid that is left is fine for feeding to pigs or poultry.

ROYAL FANS (SHORTCAKE)

¾ cup butter   2 cups flour
½ cup brown sugar

Mix butter and sugar together; add flour little by little; pat resulting dough in 8-inch round. Bake in oven (about 375°) till crisp. While still hot, cut in 8 fan-shaped pieces.

I am not giving recipes for crumpets, saffron, or fruit cake. I have a recipe for crumpets, but I've never tried it since I have usually been able to buy them already cooked and only had to toast them. I have no recipe for saffron cake because I never liked the stuff, and I haven't bothered about the fruit cake because there are dozens of recipes in every cookbook. The only difference between mine and others is that I never put in any lemon or orange peel or cherries. I occasionally add dates.

The final recipe I give is that mentioned on page 91.

CHOCOLATE PIE SUPREME
Crust

2 squares chocolate	⅔ cup confectioners' sugar
2 tablespoons butter	1½ cups ground almonds or
2 tablespoons hot water	flaked coconut

Melt chocolate and butter in double boiler. Mix hot water and sugar. Stir into chocolate mixture. Add almonds or coconut and mix well. Grease *well* a 9-inch pie plate and press mixture along sides and bottom evenly. Chill till hard (an hour should more than do it).

Filling

1 envelope gelatin	3 eggs, separated
1 cup sugar	1 teaspoon vanilla or almond
½ teaspoon salt	extract
1⅓ cups milk	Pinch of cream of tartar
2 teaspoons instant coffee	½ cup heavy cream
3 squares semisweet chocolate	

Mix gelatin, ½ cup of the sugar, salt, milk, and coffee in double boiler. Add chocolate and cook over boiling water until chocolate and gelatin are melted. Remove from heat and stir till mixture is blended. Beat egg yolks slightly, pour in chocolate mixture, and stir quickly. Return to double boiler and cook till mixture thickens (about 5 minutes). Pour into bowl. Add vanilla or almond extract. Chill till mixture begins to jell and mounds slightly when gently heaped with a spoon. Beat egg whites with cream of tartar till frothy. Add remaining sugar a little at a time and beat till stiff. Fold into chocolate mixture. Whip cream till thick and glossy and fold in also. Pour into pie shell and leave in refrigerator until firm. If you want to gild the lily, add a topping of whipped cream flavored with almond or vanilla. To detach from pan, pass pan slowly over burner.

I have never known exactly what "fatty degeneration of the heart" was, but it sounds like the sort of thing overindulgence in any of the above might bring on. Therefore, like notices on cigarette advertising, I say *caution*. However, none of the dishes mentioned above are suitable for the addition of lethal ingredients.

So—*bon appétit!*